DEAD **R**

A Review of Horror and the...
Edited by Alex Houstoun and Michael J. Abolafia

No. 26 (Fall 2019)

3 A Cultic Gathering .... Darrell Schweitzer

6 Trio of Terrors... Greg Gbur
   Larry Blamire, *More Tales of the Callamo Mountains*; Orrin
   Grey, *Guignol and Other Sardonic Tales*; Lucy A. Snyder,
   Garden of Eldritch Delights.

11 The Curated Repast of Subdivisions .... The Joey Zone
   Ann and Jeff Vandermeer, *The Big Book of Classic Fantasy*.

14 "The Most Poignant Sensations of My Existence": Visiting
   the Ladd Observatory at NecronomiCon Providence ....
   Karen Joan Kohoutek

16 Two Writers: Lives and Works .... S. T. Joshi
   Mike Ashley, *Starlight Man: The Extraordinary Life of Algernon
   Blackwood*; William F. Nolan, *Writing as Life: Selected Essays of
   William F. Nolan*, ed. Jason V Brock.

24 Ramsey's Rant: Volumes of Volumes .... Ramsey Campbell

31 Sing Your Sadness Deep, Laura Mauro........ Daniel Pietersen
   Laura Mauro, *Sing Your Sadness Deep*.

34 Man as a Mystery.................................. Donald Sidney-Fryer
   Arthur Machen, *Collected Fiction*, ed. S. T. Joshi: Volume I:
   1888–1895; Volume II: 1896–1610; Volume III: 1911–1937;
   Mark Valentine and Timothy J. Jarvis, ed., *The Secret
   Ceremonies: Critical Essays on Arthur Machen*.

40 The Unseen, Quiet Dark .... Fiona Maeve Geist
   Michael Kelly, *All the Things We Never See*.

43 Curtains of the Impossible: A Remembrance of Sam
   Gafford .... Farah Rose Smith

47 A New Take on the Chambers Mythos .... Acep Hale
   Brian Hauser, *Memento Mori: The Fathomless Shadows*.

53 Ars Necronomica 2019: What Drives the Dark Dreams of
   That Divine City?.. Michelle Souliere

64 Delicate, Collectible Screams .... Géza A. G. Reilly
Thomas Ligotti, *A Little White Book of Screams and Whispers.*

67 "When Blue Meets Yellow in the West":
Stranger Things 3 .... Hank Wagner and Bev Vincent

77 Train Reading .... Peter Cannon

79 My NecronomiCon 2019: Wanderings and Wonders ....
Elena Tchougounova-Paulson

81 The Rocky Beginnings of *Weird Tales* ...... Darrell Schweitzer
John Locke, *The Thing's Incredible! The Secret Origins of* Weird Tales.

86 Sam Gafford and Ulthar Press .... S. T. Joshi
Farah Rose Smith, ed. *Machinations and Mesmerism: Tales Inspired by E. T. A. Hoffmann.*

91 "I No Longer Live in This House": The Liminality of Undeath in the Works of R. Murray Gilchrist .... Daniel Pietersen

98 Fathoms of Tropes .... Géza A. G. Reilly
Frogwares, *The Sinking City.*

101 Were We Ever Innocent? Childhood Horrors of Knowledge and Sexuality in Gene Wolfe's Fiction .... Marc Aramini

114 "We Make Ourselves out of Stories, Y'Know?" ....
Karen Joan Kohoutek
Eric J. Guignard, *Doorways to the Deadeye.*

117 Recollections on NecronomiCon 2019 ...... Edward Guimont

119 You Know Who the Monster Is .... Michael D. Miller
S. L. Edwards, *Whiskey and Other Unusual Ghosts.*

124 Loving Horror Films Too Much .... Acep Hale
Jon Kitley, *Discover the Horror: One Man's Quest for Monsters, Maniacs, and the Meaning of It All.*

131 Haters and Devotees Alike: NecronomiCon 2019 ....
Geza A. G. Reilly

133 About the Contributors

DEAD RECKONINGS is published by Hippocampus Press, P.O. Box 641, New York, NY 10156 (www.hippocampuspress.com). Copyright © 2019 by Hippocampus Press. Cover art by Jason C. Eckhardt. Cover design by Barbara Briggs Silbert. Hippocampus Press logo by Anastasia Damianakos. Orders and subscriptions should be sent to Hippocampus Press. Contact Alex Houstoun at deadreckoningsjournal@gmail.com for assignments or before submitting a publication for review.

ISSN 1935-6110   ISBN 978-1-61498-288-3

A Cultic Gathering

Darrell Schweitzer

"You look exhausted," someone said to me as I sat down behind my table in the Vendors' Room on the third day of NecronomiCon Providence 2019. "Ah," I replied, "I shall revive. Having people fling money at me has wonderful restorative properties."

Well, it was exhausting and, not to put too much of an emphasis on the money-making aspect of it, I did spend a great deal of time behind a dealer's table at NecronomiCon, as my intended roommate had to cancel due to a knee injury and I had no one to assist me. That meant when I was on a panel I had to throw a blanket over the table and put out a sign that I would be back soon. (The programming at this convention, both the panels and the academic track, is generally excellent.) There *is* a commercial aspect to NecronomiCon, undeniably. Lovecraftians, if you have the right material, spend money like water. I was mostly selling my own titles and Lovecraft-related material like *Weirdbook* and *Weird Tales* magazines and Wildside Press editions of Robert E. Howard and Lord Dunsany. It was a huge success. I do note that this year the majority of the tables seemed to feature small-press publications or non-book items like T-shirts, jewelry, and idols. It is a great place to pick up idols. Last time, in 2017, I bartered some books for a very fine Dagon, which I keep in my office in an eldritch shrine, next to various Cthulhus. There is an opening for a well-stocked antiquarian bookseller. I saw only saw two Arkham Houses books in the room. This is a far cry from the NecronomiCons of old, in which a colleague had the best convention he'd ever experienced and *then* made an extra seven thousand dollars at the last minute when a German, who had been agonizing over it all weekend, broke down and bought *The Outsider and Others, Beyond the Wall of Sleep,* and something else in that range—I think it was Clark Ashton Smith's *The Dark Chateau*. Nobody had such rarities this year.

But enough of this talk of lucre. NecronomiCon is a gathering of the cultists, where Lovecraftians from all over the world can meet one another. The core experience of any such convention is not only getting together with old friends, but really good book talk, such as I had at an off-site party with Guest of Honor Peter Cannon and Pulitzer-winning critic Michael Dirda. The convention comes together on shared interests, on our love of Lovecraft and weird fiction.

There were receptions, including a particularly fine one at the Providence Art Club, which is just up the three for the Fleur de Lys building where the student who made the bass-relief in "The Call of Cthulhu" once resided. The College Hill neighborhood is full of such Lovecraftian sites, so, yes, of course there were walking tours. I have conducted them in the past, though I did not quite feel up to it this time, in the sweltering August heat, and in any case I was much too busy having money flung at me (see above) during the daytime.

I cut out of the Art Club reception early and because I did not want to miss Robert Lloyd Parry's reading/performance as M. R. James. Parry is an English actor who assumes the persona of James and partially tells, partially acts the stories. I saw/heard him do "'Oh, Whistle, and I'll Come to You, My Lad'" and "The Ash-Tree." Brilliant stuff. I also saw a live performance of the H. P. Lovecraft Historical Society's radio play of "The Lurking Fear," likewise not to be missed.

For me the climax of any NecronomiCon is the Prayer Breakfast Sunday morning. I arrive looking my ecclesiastical best in a black robe with skeletal bones on it (taken from a Grim Reaper costume) a red fez with a Cthulhu patch, and a necklace of tiny bone skulls. I am choir master, having written the hymns ("Let's Gibber Now of Yog-Sothoth," "We Will Raise Him Up," etc.), but much credit must go to Sister Faye Ringel, who plays the keyboard and is actually musically trained, thus able to keep the Amorphous Tabernacle Choir more or less shambling (or croaking) in the same direction. This year's services were highlighted by a hilarious Lovecraftian rap performance by Cody Goodfellow, Anthony Teth, and Scott R. Jones. After that, back to the vendor's table for another ordeal of flung money. I always regret missing the after-con ceremonies at HPL's grave in nearby Swann Point Cemetery, since I cannot get loaded up and out of there for at least an hour or more after closing.

An eldritch time was had by all. We come away spiritually renewed, and waiting until the stars are again right, as they are in odd-numbered years. On to 2021.

Trio of Terrors

Greg Gbur

LARRY BLAMIRE. *More Tales of the Callamo Mountains.* n.p.: Bookaroonie Press, 2017. 206 pages. $19.45 tpb. ISBN 978-0-557005-64-2.

ORRIN GREY. *Guignol and Other Sardonic Tales.* Petaluma, CA: Word Horde, 2018. 240 pages. $15.99 tpb. ISBN 978-1-939905-42-0.

LUCY A. SNYDER. *Garden of Eldritch Delights.* Bowie, MD: Raw Dog Screaming Press, 2018. 184 pages. $14.95 tpb. ISBN 978-1-947879-08-9.

I often find it quite refreshing to take a step back in my horror explorations to appreciate the wealth and variety of horror fiction available today. Thanks to small publishers, independent publishers, and self-publishers, a lot more work is seeing the light of day that historically—some decades ago—would have been neglected by the larger presses. With this in mind, here we take a look at three collections of short fiction that have come out over the past year and a half—a trio of terrors—that illustrate the delightful variety of tone and subject matter one can find in horror fiction. The only unifying characteristic of the collections discussed here, by Larry Blamire, Orrin Grey, and Lucy A. Snyder, is that all the authors are people whose work I first became familiar with through social media, another modern tool that can help us find excellent fiction to lose ourselves in.

Larry Blamire is best known for his 2001 cult classic movie *Lost Skeleton of Cadavra* and its sequel, which he wrote, directed, and starred in. The movies are a simultaneous parody of and homage to the low-budget sci-fi and horror B-movies of the 1950s and their charming naïveté. But Blamire has also ventured into serious horror with two self-published collections, the 2008 collection *Tales of the Callamo Mountains* and the fan-requested 2017 follow-up, *More Tales of the Callamo*

Mountains. These collections demonstrate that he can cause a chill as well as draw a laugh. Both volumes may be categorized as Western horror, and are set in the fictional and titular Callamo Mountains, a remote wilderness in which many inexplicable and horrifying things happen. The Callamo Mountains serve as a character in and of themselves, much like W. H. Pugmire's classic Sesqua Valley and H. P. Lovecraft's Miskatonic country.

Blamire's tales hearken back to a time when our understanding of the world and the frontier was limited, and the greatest thing to fear was what might be waiting for you right over the next hill. The stories have the atmosphere of classic folklore, often simply recounting something very unpleasant that happened to someone, sometime, with no underlying moral other than the fact that the world is a terrifying, inexplicable place. One particular talent of Blamire is his ability to take very ordinary characters and place them in extraordinary, even impossible, situations. In the tale "Bar None," a ranch hand in the wilderness finds himself suddenly face to face with a beautiful woman in an elegant gown, who slowly walks toward him without a word. Much of the dread of the tales comes from trying to imagine how one would react if faced with a similar impossible situation.

Both collections are filled with excellent stories; here I mention only a few of my favorites from the latter collection of fourteen tales. In "The Arrest of Mr. Pollamer," a celebrated contortionist is implicated in a gruesome murder. When the local deputies attempt to bring him in for questioning, they find that there is much more to the man and his abilities than meets the eye, and the revelation leads to dire consequences. In "The Valley of Capper Crabb," two prospectors enter the titular valley in search of gold. They assume the valley is abandoned but find the home of Crabb, who demands payment for each day they remain in the valley to prospect. At first the cost is quite reasonable, but every day the price goes up dramatically, until the men are faced with a terrible choice. In "Heliograph No. 24," my favorite of the collection, soldiers stationed on distant mountaintops use heliographs—light flashers—to communicate via Morse code. But Station 23 notices something indistinguishable approaching Station 24, and soon after the messages from Station 24 become increasingly erratic, cryptic, and ominous, building toward some sort of revelation.

Blamire's artistic vision, it is worth noting, extends to the cover art of the books, which was done by the author himself. These covers, which stand as short tales in their own right, are also a reminder of those bits of folklore passed down orally through families and amongst friends and coworkers.

Orrin Grey draws much of his inspiration from different classic sources: H. P. Lovecraft and his contemporaries, but more significantly the monster movies of the 1950s to the 1970s, from the rampaging Japanese kaiju to the creeping and lumbering monsters of Universal Pictures to the works of Roger Corman and Hammer Films. Grey has become an active and well-recognized writer of short horror fiction, and his work has appeared in countless anthologies, including Ellen Datlow's *Best Horror of the Year*. His previous collections include *Never Bet the Devil and Other Warnings* (2012; reprinted in a premium edition in 2017) and *Painted Monsters and Other Strange Beasts* (2015).

In his most recent collection of fourteen tales, *Guignol and Other Sardonic Tales* (2018), Grey displays the same love of those classic monster movies but with modern twists. Nostalgia is often a key element in the stories, not necessary to enjoy them but adding to their enjoyment for those familiar with the references. In "Invaders of Gla'aki," two young friends become obsessed with completing a very strange arcade game at their local convenience store, even though success may have quite hideous consequences. In "Baron von Werewolf Presents: Frankenstein Against the Phantom Planet," a Sunday Creature Feature television presenter gives the children viewing a rare treat: a showing of an almost unheard-of stop-motion animated film from the *King Kong* era. The showing, however, comes at a cost greater than licensing rights. In "The Cult of the Headless Men," my favorite in the collection, a struggling horror filmmaker visits his friend's ancestral home in England, with the goal of transitioning it to the new *Dark*

Shadows style of Gothic horror. But a professor has been living on the estate for years, finishing his anthropological studies on a remote island tribe, and the revelations he brings will threaten not only the film production, but the lives of all present.

It should be noted that not every story uses classic entertainment nostalgia as a vehicle. In the modern fairy tale "The Blue Light," a soldier returning from war stumbles upon an unexpected power, and he uses it to overturn the societal order. In "The Well and the Wheel," a woman returning to her late father's home learns the terrible secret of how he kept her safe through the years.

One aspect of Grey's stories that will strike the reader is how fun they are. They capture that thrill of discovering the inherent weirdness and imagination of the horror genre for the first time, of experiencing events that might actually happen if our reality were just a little different. In this collection, however, Grey's work also has an extra bit of intensity, and even cruelty. This is hinted at by the titular reference to the Grand Guignol, the nineteenth-century French theater at which horrifying acts of violence were simulated. As Grey notes in his afterword, however, cruelty and fun can coexist, at least in fiction.

Much darker in tone is Lucy A. Snyder's *Garden of Eldritch Delights,* a compilation of a dozen stories that often mix horror, science fiction, and fantasy in unusual ways. This is the eighth collection of short fiction by the prolific Snyder, who has also written a trio of novels and the nonfiction *Shooting Yourself in the Head For Fun and Profit: A Writer's Survival Guide*.

As in her previous collection, *While the Black Stars Burn* (2015), Snyder often draws upon Lovecraftian cosmic horror, but puts a more human and tragic face on the characters and their struggles. In "Sunset on Mott Island," a woman must contend with her dying mother as well as her own illness while facing the end of the world. In "The Gentleman Caller," a disabled woman working as a phone sex operator gains an unusual power—but that power comes with unexpected and apocalyptic consequences. In "The Yellow Death," a woman's sister makes a surprising reappearance in her life, long after humanity has been devastated by a plague of seeming vampires.

Other stories in the collection cross genres in innovative ways. In "Fraeternal," twin siblings find that they have the power together to control their destiny, past and future, but run into fundamental disagreements as to how that should be done. In "A Noble Endeavor," a plantation slave is forced to work in the laboratory of a cruel mad scientist, and her actions could change the course of history. Science fiction and Lovecraft cross paths in "Blossoms Blackened Like Dead Stars," as humanity seeks to retaliate against the cosmic horrors that have attacked Earth. The counterattack, however, could cost more than any human is willing to give. The title character of the fantasy tale "A Hero of Grünjord" manages to repel otherworldly invaders but finds an even greater challenge in dealing with the attachments of her past.

In reading *Garden of Eldritch Delights,* my impression is that most of the stories share a common feeling of despair, and each tale features characters coping with that despair in different ways. The protagonist in "Sunset on Mott Island" finds solace in mundane routine, while the protagonist in "The Gentleman Caller" uses escapism to cope with the challenges of her life. The result is a collection of stories that is emotionally dark and powerful, a strong illustration of how Lovecraft's original ideas of cosmic horror can be employed to tell stories with very different themes.

The three collections discussed here, by Blamire, Grey, and Snyder, are all excellent, and nicely illustrate the variety of tones and themes that can be found in today's horror.

The Curated Repast of Subdivisions

The joey Zone

ANN and JEFF VANDERMEER. *The Big Book of Classic Fantasy*. New York: Vintage Books, 2019. 822 pp. $25.00 tpb. ISBN: 978-0-525-43556-3.

"The most painful part of the experience was reading Salvador Dali's fiction."

—@jeffvandermeer, 25 September 2018

"A night at the end of June, a child takes a walk with his mother. It's raining falling stars. The child picks up one and carries it in the palms of his hands. At home he deposits it on the table and locks it in a reversed glass. The next morning, getting up, he lets escape a scream of terror: A worm, during the night has nibbled his star!"

—According to Dali, written by him at age 8

The above is provided as a public service in the interest of giving an even more complete survey than included in this *Big Book*.

Painful? We've read worse assuredly. While nothing is as brief as this in this volume, it would not be out of its scope. There are ninety selections, not all of which are complete narratives (nine novels are excerpted, ranging from *Through the Looking-Glass* to *The Night Land*). Twelve of the authors appeared previously in the Vandermeers' collection *The Weird* (2011). *The Big Book* in some respects presents a deeper cut of that aesthetic. One story, Hagiwara Sakutaro's "The Town of Cats," is in both anthologies.

Regular subscribers to this journal might first associate the term "fantasy" with a heroic narrative in a "secondary world," either in an epic (think Tolkien) or in a pulpier, shorter form (think Howard). Both the Oxford professor and Two-Gun Bob are in these pages. The Vandermeers define *Classic* Fantasy as that written "from the early 1800s to World War II, from the start of a nascent idea of 'fantasy' as opposed to 'folktale.'" There are folk and fairytale tropes abounding in these pages due to "the rate of fey" the editors use in establishing parameters for this collection, but many extend Beyond the Fields We Knew.

There is a preponderance of playful comic fantasy, the welcome example being Oscar Wilde's delightful "The Remarkable Rocket"; a rather overdone choice, on the other hand, is Gustav Meyrink's "Blamol." Franz Blei's "The Big Bestiary of Modern Literature" is doted on and not surprisingly, as it seems a formative influence on the anthologists' Thackery Lambshead books and *Kosher Guide to Imaginary Animals*.

Science fantasy—another subdivision—is represented by Edgar Allan Poe's "M. Valdemar" and Fitz James O'Brien's "The Diamond Lens." "The Masque of the Red Death" or "The Wondersmith" come to mind as more suitable examples from either, however. And while this reviewer loves the writing of Bruno Schulz, "A Night of the High Season," while written fantastically in style and descriptions, does not have anything fantastic happen in it per se. (The same also goes for Herman Melville and his tale "The Tartarus of Maids.") "Too much time and energy has been expended by well-meaning editors of past anthologies invoking such arguments as the 'Nathaniel Hawthorne Defense' to establish fantasy's bona fides." The Vandermeers then proceed to do just that themselves, recently admitting in a recent interview something akin to a "we speak to repatriate" the "literary" into the "fantastical"—is there a need to boost the relevance of the latter?

We must look at what this book is rather than what it is not. Jeff Vandermeer's predilection for speculative fictions concerned with humanity's interaction with the natural world and its flora and fauna infuse an underlying flavor to this self-described "sumptuous repast." The will-o'-the-wisps of the Hans Christian Andersen story cry, "they are drowning our meadows and drying them up! What will become of our descendants?" Jasoomian Imperialist John Carter takes up longsword in the extract from Edgar Rice Burroughs's Mars series to fight the "hideous," "repulsive" *plant* men.

And yet. There are samples from *The Worm Ouroboros* or *A Voyage to Arcturus* to entice an uninitiated palate desiring refinement. A new encounter was with the writing of Marcel Schwob, his standout story (complete with climate change!) being "The Death of Odjigh," reminiscent of J. H. Rosny. And any time an anthology contains a selection by Leonora Carrington it is worth a read. In summation: While not the definitive collection of fantasy—classic or otherwise—this book's value lies in its relation to the amount of material that was new to me. For now, this far-encompassing, albeit curated, tour will last long enough for a night at the end of June.

"The Most Poignant Sensations of My Existence": Visiting the Ladd Observatory at NecronomiCon Providence

Karen Joan Kohoutek

As in previous years, NecronomiCon Providence 2019 was so jam-packed, I couldn't possibly do everything I planned to do. I managed to fit in several thought-provoking panels, an outdoor rave with costumed shoggoths, my first trip to the Swan Point Cemetery in many years, and, of course, meeting up with friends old and new. My personal highlight, though, was undoubtedly a visit to the Ladd Observatory.

The observatory is normally only open to the public on Tuesdays, and I was unsure if I'd ever manage to get there, so I was giddy when it was opened up for us as part of the NecronomiCon bus tours. Maintained in its historical condition by Brown University's Physics Department, the Ladd Observatory is both intimate and far-reaching. Originally opened in 1891, it still looks and feels very much like a place from the past. Relatively small inside, it is full of antique equipment, and the windows in the reading room where Lovecraft would have sat, pondering the cosmos, look out onto a quiet, leafy neighborhood.

We were welcomed by its curator, historian Michael Umbricht, who showed us around and let us go up the narrow stairs to the observation floor, where he used old-fashioned rope pulleys to open the dome above the telescope, something that must be truly amazing at night.

Lovecraft's relationship with the study of astronomy is one of the points that, for me, most humanizes him, making him a relatable person. I too once thought I was going to study astronomy, although for me it was the Periodical Table of Elements, along with the math, that put the kibosh on my dreamed-of career at NASA. A poetically based interest in the infinity above us is very different from the kind of calculations and orientation toward hard science needed to devote oneself fully to the discipline, as the weird bard of Providence and I both learned.

In general, I disapprove of the idea of trauma as inspiration, but being here made me wonder. How much was it the destruction of Lovecraft's dream that forced him to channel his cosmic aspirations into fiction? If he had gone to college, gotten a job making astronomical observations and teaching the basics of the universe to students . . . would he have written the stories that brought us to NecronomiCon? What would he have preferred?

As it is, the Ladd Observatory is a tangible piece of Lovecraft's life, more or less as it appeared in his time. It's a real place, where he spent time as a real person, doing things and wanting things, before he became a kind of icon. This entry point into the past, and the uncanniness of history, is also dedicated to the larger universe. It opens up to the cosmos, to ideas that are both intellectual and inspirational, representing part of the appeal of the weird: reaching out for the sublime, but always back-dropped by the darkness.

Two Writers: Lives and Works

S. T. Joshi

MIKE ASHLEY. *Starlight Man: The Extraordinary Life of Algernon Blackwood*. Eureka, CA: Stark House Press, 2019. 462 pp. $22.95 tpb. ISBN 978-1-944520-64-9.
WILLIAM F. NOLAN. *Writing as Life: Selected Essays of William F. Nolan*. Edited by Jason V Brock. Portland, OR: Dark Regions Press, 2019. 292 pp. $20.00 (tpb: 978-1-62641-291-0), $75.00 (signed/limited hardcover).

The lives of most writers tend to be rather uninteresting—for the simple reason that they spend most of their waking hours writing. But the writers to be considered here—one a towering classic of weird fiction, the other a monumental figure in his own right and, thankfully, still with us—defy that stereotype. Both writers were (and are) incredibly prolific; and yet, both have managed to cram a remarkable amount of activity into their lives, oftentimes in realms well beyond their areas of literary focus. Of the two books under review, one is an account of the author by a pioneering and tenacious biographer; in the other, the author himself provides glimpses of his multifaceted life and career.

Mike Ashley's *Starlight Man* first appeared in 2001, published by Constable in England under its current title and in the U.S. by Carroll & Graf under the title *Algernon Blackwood: An Extraordinary Life*. Ashley was forced to trim the book at that time, and in this reprint he has restored those cuts, as well as added a wealth of new information. The result is, after a full forty years of biographical and literary research, the most exhaustive, sympathetic, and penetrating chronicle of this enigmatic writer that anyone is ever likely to write.

It would be cumbrous to recount, even in the broadest strokes, the life and work of Algernon Blackwood (1869–1951). He was the son of Stevenson Arthur Blackwood, a distinguished political figure who would become Secretary to the

Post Office. But more significantly, Blackwood's father joined the evangelical movement of the period, and the young Blackwood remembered being terrified of the fires of hell. On the whole, however, he had a relatively happy childhood. He attended various schools, including a year (1885–86) spent at the school of the Moravian Brotherhood in Königsfeld, Germany. Ashley presents evidence that Blackwood actually had a relatively good time here, in spite of the school's austerity, so that its portrayal as a haven for devil-worshippers in the story "Secret Worship" is a bit puzzling.

As a teenager Blackwood stumbled upon a copy of *Yogi Aphorisms* by Bhagwan Shree Patanjali. This tract afforded Blackwood a much-needed antidote to his father's fire-and-brimstone teachings and also fused with the love of nature that he had already absorbed. He read other works of Eastern philosophy and esoterism, although he never became a full-fledged "occultist." While, over the years, he did investigate some haunted houses under the informal aegis of the Society for Psychical Research, he retained a healthy skepticism regarding claims of supernatural incursion. He also gained a lifelong interest in theosophy and reincarnation.

A visit to Canada with his father led to Blackwood's decision to move there in 1890. He attempted to run a dairy farm, but his complete absence of business acumen led to its failure. Drifting down to New York, he became a reporter for the *New York Sun*. He had done some writing and editing by this time, but clearly did not envision authorship as a career. In New York he fell under the influence of a suave con artist, George Arthur Bigge, who repeatedly stole what little money he had. Blackwood's extreme poverty, and his victimization by Bigge, are vividly chronicled in *Episodes Before Thirty* (1923), where Bigge is disguised as "Boyde." At various points Blackwood was actually a vagrant. Things began to turn for the better when he became a reporter for the *New York Times* (1895–97) and then, oddly, took a position as the private secretary of a wealthy banker, James Speyer. But although Blackwood took several trips to Canada to get away from the filthy urban metropolis of New York, he eventually became homesick and returned to England in 1899.

It was only now that he began writing fiction in earnest. Ashley makes plain that nearly the entirety of Blackwood's output is patently autobiographical. His trips to Canada inspired "The Wendigo" and other tales; his work for Speyer led to the writing of "The Strange Adventures of a Private Secretary in New York"; and, most vividly, a canoe trip down the Danube, in the company of Wilfrid Wilson, inspired "The Willows."

Blackwood briefly joined the Hermetic Order of the Golden Dawn, and also became acquainted with another great author of weird fiction, Arthur Machen; but the two writers, interestingly enough, disliked each other's work. (Machen thought Blackwood's work too mystical; Blackwood, late in life, merely stated that Machen's tales "left no special mark on me.") Blackwood's career took a remarkable turn when he met a friend, Angus Hamilton, who read some of his stories and immediately took them to the publisher Eveleigh Nash, who agreed to publish then. *The Empty House and Other Ghost Stories* appeared in 1906, followed by *The Listener and Other Stories* in 1907.

John Silence—Physician Extraordinary (1908) became a bestseller thanks to a clever advertising campaign, and the income thus received allowed Blackwood to spend most of the next six years in Switzerland. As Ashley correctly remarks, "The next five years would see Blackwood produce the most remarkable body of supernatural fiction ever written." This included the novels *The Education of Uncle Paul* (1909), *The Human Chord* (1910), and *The Centaur* (1911), and the story collections *The Lost Valley and Other Stories* (1910), *Pan's Garden* (1912), and *Incredible Adventures* (1914). Once again, these novels are infused with autobiographical elements. *Uncle Paul* is to my mind comparable to the *Alice* books and *The Wind in the Willows* as a fantasy for (and about) children. Blackwood's hermetic studies led to *The Human Chord*, a novel dealing with the possibility of a quartet of singers who might dissolve the fabric of the universe. *The Centaur* is Blackwood's spiritual autobiography, transforming his trip to Sicily, Constantinople, and the Caucasus region of Russia into a throbbingly vital novel about the spiritual powers of nature. Trips to Egypt inspired "Sand" (in *Pan's Garden*), "A Descent into Egypt" (in *Incredible Adventures*), and other tales.

By this time Blackwood had met Maya Stuart-King, the wife of the wealthy Russian businessman Baron Johann Knoop. Many of his books for the next decade or so are dedicated to "M. S.-K." Blackwood, a lifelong bachelor, developed several platonic but intense relationships with women over his lifetime, and none more intense than with Maya. His reincarnation novel *The Wave* (1916) is largely about his curious involvement with the Knoops. Ashley has a higher opinion of another novel published at this time, *Julius LeVallon* (1916), than I do, but it is nonetheless a powerful vehicle for Blackwood's expression of his faith in the regenerative powers of nature.

The rest of Blackwood's long life need not be gone into in detail—although Ashley does exactly that, and compellingly so. He tells of Blackwood's writing of other fantasies for adults and children, notably *A Prisoner in Fairyland* (1913), which was turned into a musical, *The Starlight Express* (1915), with music by Edward Elgar. The production was not a particular success and was largely panned by critics, but for the rest of his life Blackwood hoped to see a revival of this work, in which he had a great emotional stake. It is rather sad to think that in the remaining years of his life Blackwood would generate no literary work even remotely comparable to what he had done in his first decade as a full-time writer; in this he curiously parallels Ray Bradbury. But that early work is so remarkable that Blackwood's attempts to recapture its magic must be forgiven.

Ashley also has a high opinion of *The Bright Messenger* (1921), an avowed sequel to *Julius LeVallon,* but I am not convinced that this work amounts to much. Both novels deal with the idea that the human race can somehow be re-infused with spirituality by a return to nature; but the later novel, written after World War I, all too plangently betrays Blackwood's despair over the fate of humanity and undermines the cheerful message he is attempting to convey. It is engaging to see that Blackwood actually served as a kind of spy during the war, trying to unearth information on German war plans while posing as a tourist in Switzerland.

After the war, Blackwood fell under the spell of the scientific mystic Georgei Gurdjieff and his colleague P. D. Ouspensky; but around this time he admitted that he had pretty much said what he had to say as a writer. He focused on books for children: *Sambo and Snitch* (1927), *Dudley and Gilderoy* (1929), *The Fruit Stoners* (1934), and others. Some of these are quite charming, but they remain insubstantial. In 1934 he began a new career, doing broadcasts on BBC radio. In 1936 he was involved in the BBC's first public television broadcast. He continued this work during World War II. He came close to death when, on October 13, 1940, his London house was hit by a German bomb during the blitz. He survived, but many of his papers and correspondence were lost.

It is difficult, short of superlatives, to convey the brilliance of Mike Ashley's biography. He has meticulously researched not only Blackwood's own life and work, but also the lives of those many individuals—ranging from family members to fellow writers to other individuals (such as the famous actor Henry Ainley and his family, with whom Blackwood lived for a time)—who were central to Blackwood's existence. Ashley's summaries of Blackwood's novels and tales are so enticing that they tempt one to drop his book and plunge into the works in question. His assessment of Blackwood's work is on the whole judicious, and he has a clear-eyed view of both the virtues and flaws of his writing.

What few blemishes there are in this book relate to matters of style, grammar, punctuation, and so forth. Impressive as Ashley is as a scholar, critic, editor, and historian, he is one who needs a little help with his prose; and his publisher has neglected to provide it. His book is sprinkled with grammatical errors ("principle" [noun] for "principal" [adjective]; "it's" for "its"; "lead" for "led"; "disassociated" for "dissociated") and poor punctuation. And his publisher has done him no favors by a failure (one that could have been corrected by a single click of the mouse) to begin footnote numbers anew with each chapter; instead, by the end of the book we have footnotes numbering in the 500s. These are, as I say, minuscule blemishes in an otherwise exemplary work; but they are blemishes all the same.

Algernon Blackwood died just at the time when the American writer William F. Nolan (b. 1928) was beginning his literary career. He published a chapbook, *Ray Bradbury Review* (1952), that constituted the first critical assessment of that writer, who had been writing professionally for only about a decade. *Writing as Life* is not in any sense a formal autobiography, nor even a memoir; indeed, it explicitly declares itself to be a collection of Nolan's best essays. And yet, it is infused with autobiographical vignettes, featuring several "autobiographical pauses" that illuminate aspects of Nolan's life and beliefs beyond what the essays themselves supply.

William F. Nolan must be tired of being labelled "the author of *Logan's Run*." He is the diametrical opposite of the one-book author: he has written horror, fantasy, and science fiction; he has written biographies of John Huston, Steve McQueen, Dashiell Hammett, and other figures; he has written screenplays, essays, journalism, book reviews; he has even written some highly creditable poetry. This book recounts the many influences, literary and otherwise, that have led to his incredibly diverse output. Its opening essays delightfully tell of his upbringing in an Irish district of Kansas City, where the youngster fell under the sway of superhero comics (Batman was his chosen favorite; he scorned Superman and also thought Lois Lane "the world's dumbest female, since she couldn't tell [Clark] Kent was really Superman behind those glasses").

Nolan didn't like the TV shows or movies based upon the superhero comics ("Comic heroes belonged in the comics"), but he did become fascinated with the old-time Westerns. These films were hugely popular in the 1930s and 1940s, but died out in the next decade; for Nolan, however, "the Western lives on, at least in my memories." This interest may have led to his passion for the writer Frederick Faust, who revolutionized the Western story under the pseudonym Max Brand. Nolan's essay on Brand in this book ("Western Giant") is a remarkably vivid portrayal of a writer who, because of his almost inconceivable prolificity, would otherwise be dismissed as a pulp hack. But Faust's training in classical literature and mythology led to the infusion of mythic elements into his Westerns; one critic referred to him as "the Homer of the Western story."

Nolan also developed a lifelong love of racing, and his essay on a 1908 race from New York to Paris (heading west, through the United States, Canada, and Russia) is riveting. Another essay, on the 1960 Grand Prix race in Monte Carlo, is also stirring, displaying to the full Nolan's powers of description:

> The competing cars roll smoothly into position on the bannered quay front, forming seven rows. The sky is overcast and sunless; a grossly distended cloud over the Alpes Maritimes presages rain. The waters of the Mediterranean lap quietly against the gray, monolithic stones outside the harbor entrance. Date palms stir faintly, and the scarlet Riviera flowers burn against the cool green of the casino gardens. Multicolored villas and apartments dot the cliffs, rising in steps like an immense layer cake above the streets.

Nolan himself ran in a race sponsored by the Road Race Training Association, as related in another essay.

One of the most striking passages of this book relates to Nolan's Catholic upbringing. He tells the appalling story that, because his mother had married a divorced man, she was obliged—under threat of excommunication—to refrain from sexual relations with him! "Part of the deal was that she and Dad would never again sleep in the same room, be in a state of undress in front of each other, or indulge in any physical affection beyond a simple (and nonsexual) kiss." Nolan rightly condemns this as "a prime example of religious blackmail and a perversion of normal human relations," and it leads to his avowal that he is now an "anti-Catholic."

Several of the essays in the book are not autobiographical at all. A long piece maintaining that John Dillinger didn't die in a shootout with the Feds in 1934 is certainly an interesting foray into revisionist history; I am unable to assess the merits of its arguments, but it makes for engaging reading. Nolan writes poignantly of Ernest Hemingway's last years, plagued by ill-health and depression, leading to his suicide. Long essays on Bradbury and Richard Matheson, both of whom he has known since the 1950s, are substantial but relatively routine; the piece on Matheson is, in effect, a fusion of essay and interview. A highly entertaining piece on how he and the screenwriter Norman Corwin fared on the set of a TV show being shot in Toronto richly conveys the tortuous ways in which Hollywood seeks to create a fake reality for our entertainment.

Two writers, Algernon Blackwood and William F. Nolan, of very different sorts, united by their devotion to the cause of literature and united, too, by the fact that they have generated a body of work whose substance, richness, and distinction will allow it to endure for decades or centuries to come.

Ramsey's Rant: Volumes of Volumes

Ramsey Campbell

I've owned books ever since I can remember. My earliest recollection is of an annual I received as a Christmas present—the Rupert Bear book that is also my first memory of terror. I'd like to reminiscence about a life in books, but let me clear away some shameful truths. In my early years I had a horrid habit of reading the end before I read the tale (and an odd compulsion to reread tales whenever I found them reprinted). As my age reached double figures I fell to illustrating some of the books I owned, or more correctly defacing them with a fountain pen, possibly in emulation of Gerald Verner's anthology *Prince of Darkness,* which was illustrated with demonic woodcuts. I still possess at least one grisly bit of evidence, a volume of Dorothy L. Sayers' anthology series I scrawled in. I also had an interlude of scratching myself and dripping blood on the pages of horror books. If those copies still exist, who knows what influence they may carry? Soon I left all these practices behind, thank Thoth, and I doubt that even completist collectors will seek out the victims. Perhaps my more mature scrawls may find a buyer once I'm gone, although I'm led to wonder. When I bought a tatty paperback of *Pet Sematary* with a view to annotating it to help me write the afterword to a limited edition, it came with a stern rebuke from the bookseller for proposing to deface a book. Still, some deluded enthusiast may stump up a few coppers for the copy—time will tell, though it won't tell me. I'll justify myself by the example of my old friend Jack Sullivan, in whose books of mine I found bold annotations—"too many fire-breathing occultists", he'd noted in *The Parasite,* and I couldn't argue with his observation.

I've haunted bookshops since before I was a teenager, and I may well haunt them after my demise. I hope to be present there in print still, and may I endure in some more sentient form? Like (I suspect) many of you reading this, I've a special affection for second-hand bookshops. There's that persistent hope of finding some underpriced treasure, and I've found a few—the Museum Press *Hounds of Tindalos* for half a crown (admittedly in the early sixties) among the cheap books on the shelves outside a much-missed shop on Newington in Liverpool, a slightly rickety first edition of *Madam Crowl's Ghost* for three pounds on the highest floor of Broadhurst's splendid multi-storey Southport emporium, several Jorkens books for a few bob each in a short-lived shop just a few minutes' walk from my house.

By contrast, I'm beset by memories of items I wish I'd bought, a regret I imagine troubles some of my present readers too. Alas, my days of serious collecting are behind me, and now I prowl the dealers' rooms at conventions to ogle wistfully rather than to buy, although I fear that books are being progressively ousted from these venues, as John Brunner foresaw decades ago. I recall hearing of a copy of *The Outsider and Others* offered for a few dollars at, I think, a World Fantasy Convention—punters took it to be mispriced, but in fact it had been bound with several pages missing. A lucky buyer got there before I saw it, and I reassure myself that I have all the contents elsewhere, as is the case with most of the worthwhile fiction and verse from *Weird Tales*. I'm most troubled by the memory of dithering over a copy of Maurice Level's *Tales of Mystery and Horror* on a dealer's table at a Providence World Fantasy Convention in the eighties. Although I've little fondness for the conte cruel, and the book was priced at one hundred dollars, I was tempted by a previous owner's handwritten name on the flyleaf, but ultimately replaced the book on the table. As I type this I sigh. The name—more accurately, the famous signature—was H. P. Lovecraft, and this was presumably the copy to which he referred in *Supernatural Horror in Literature*. I do my best to content myself by recalling that I own a copy of George Sterling's *A Wine of Wizardry* in which the original owner has inscribed his name, Clark Ashton Smith.

I sometimes buy books purely for their binding—that's why I own an elaborately gilded chronicle of Westminster Abbey—but more usually for inscriptions they display, not just their content. Some contain bookplates more than a century old, denoting presentations to school pupils for good behaviour or punctuality or the like. Any old book has a history, and these exhibit more than most. The thoughts of previous owners appeal to me too. Few that I've seen rival Jack Sullivan's, but here, for instance, are two volumes of the Pan Horror series, tersely reviewed on scraps of paper tipped into the contents pages—in the case of the thirteenth volume, on the back of a postal order counterfoil made out to Cooking for Outline of Purfleet in December 1977. The tales by David Farrar and John Ware ("Spinalonga", puzzlingly listed as "'Max!'") are "rotten!!" Norman Kaufman's "Flame!" is "hot?", while the Harry Turner tale is "fair!!", and the Dulcie Gray earns no more than a question mark. A story by L. Micallef (surely a pseudonym if not an anagram) earns only "can't remember!" Norman Kaufman's contribution is "dead boring!!" and David Case's "The Dead End" is "just that" (actually the finest story in the book). At least Carl Thompson's prolonged celebration of dismemberment prompts a whoop of "whoop-peee?!!"

The fourteenth volume attracts longer comments written on a larger piece of paper. Gaylord Sabatini, that famed figure, has "The blood is the life . . ." Conrad Hill earns "Life will be the death of her . . . . .!" while Harry Turner gets "Is this the end of 'life' as we know it?" By now we may wonder if all these observations are addressed to the next reader. Myc Harrison brings only "You dirty rat . . ." but Gerald Atkins' one-page vignette generates "I ain't got nobody." David Case's lycanthropic extravaganza prompts "Kunta Kinta was never like this!!" (presumably a misspelled reference to a character in *Roots*), and Alex White's indulgence in the nastiness typical of the Pan series at its worst has "Another satisfied customer. . . . ." Myc Harrison is back to receive "Come into my parlour. . . . ." (yes, it's a spidery tale) and John Snellings' essay in cannibalism spawns "Food for thought", but Gilbert Phelps apparently warrants only "Eh?????" Here's Conrad Hill again, though both his paedophilic contribution and the comment it engenders—"Its the little things that count", mispunctuated as you see—are a pity. As for R. Chetwynd-Hayes, he or his tale "makes one glad to be a vegetarian." Puzzlingly, beneath the column of comments is written "Plus."

Sometimes irresistible curiosity prompts a purchase. For instance, how could I resist *A Man Every Inch of Him* by J. Jackson Wray (published by James Nisbet, twelfth edition, no date)? The binding shows a schoolboy in a cap, seated on a chair the wrong way round to read a book. Perhaps it's not the very volume that bears him, but he puts me in mind of a chap who has emerged from a Calvino extravaganza to illustrate his modernism. The bookplate, showing that the copy was presented to Jack Pugh at Christ Church Sunday School in Port Sunlight as second prize for regular and punctual attendance, is a bonus. The author was been a Reverend who died in 1892, and I trust he was as eccentric as his book. "Well, now, if you judge a man by his inches . . ." Who could resist such an opening line? Innocence shines through every page of the book, and so its protagonist Frank Fullerton can bid adieu to his mother by promising "I shall be back by the time the haycocks are made, and you and I will make 'sweet hay' with a vengeance"—and then, by gum, he flings his arm around her neck "and made the 'sweet' without the 'hay', by way, I suppose, go giving her a first lesson, to be improved upon at a future time." Perhaps usages have changed over the years, but I'm disconcerted by the man in blue spectacles he meets on the train to boarding school, who "took hold of Frank's fingers with one hand, and pretending to hold a rod in the other, moved it up and down as though he were working a pump-handle, and meant to fill his bucket quickly." The bespectacled fellow proves to be the headmaster, and treats Frank to a welcoming ditty in his office:

> "To be dutiful, diligent's ever the plan,
> For a boy who would like to grow into a man;
> And a hatred of wrong, and a love for the right,
> Is the way to be happy both morning and night."

It will not be his last such effusion, and Frank goes in for them as well, although he refrains from any when he wins a struggle with a bully, instead bursting into tears. Little Alfred Truscott (a fellow new boy he's protected) "came and put his little hand lovingly in the hand of his friend, and without a word they two turned away . . ." Is this naïveté about boarding-school life or realism? The author tells us that he is inclined to cry too. The headmaster can't contain himself on hearing of the incident, and declares

> "Be it boy or be it man;
> Who the quarrel first began
> Loseth credit, gaineth shame,
> And must always bear the blame."

One severe rule of the establishment is that any utterer of puns must recite a piece aloud, and one offender does. Since *The Witch and the Fairy* occupies several pages, I'll mention just that the fairy invites the young hero to "touch my rod and take my hand" before the moral is revealed: the fairy (which flies into his mouth) is Good Temper, while the banished witch is Anger. Surely none of my readers has such a wicked mind that they see anything except the moral. I'll withhold the song the boys sing while skating on a pond, but I think every one of us should keep in mind the warning the headmaster gives them:

> "If to harm you'd be a stranger,
> Always keep away from danger."

This moves the author so much that his very prose turns to verse—"I *will*, turned out ill. I *will not*, in trouble got"—at which I'll leave the rest of it. A wilful boy falls through the ice and, having cried "O Fullerton! whatever shall I do!", is duly rescued and repents. I'll spare you the chapter in which Frank sees the error of collecting birds' eggs and then deliberately flunks geography to secure the class prize for someone else. When he shares a train compartment with the prize-winner, "what pranks those two lads played in that compartment I cannot tell you," the author says, only to begin "They laid on the seats . . ." but I shall be more circumspect than he. More prankish still is Frank's bid to leap over a gleaner in a field. Old Nancy is sent sprawling but accepts his apology, although "I did feel all of a flutter like when I found myself rollin' in the stubble, with a something, I didn't know what, a scramblin' over me." With a curtsey to the headmaster she declares "He's a man, every inch of him, and if he wants another jump, he shall have another chance." Soon the justified pupils perform "a general immigration to Blanket-row, in the city of Feathersley, in the county of Beds, in the Land of Nod." Later we find Frank wrestling with his conscience, having given a wrong geography answer that the headmaster mistakes for the correct one. He confesses to the head, to be told "there's Someone else who must be told" (though you might think God already knew). Once Frank makes all well "'Dear Frank!' said Alfred Truscott, as he twined his fingers lovingly round the fingers of his friend." Far less virtuous is Molesworth—a forebear of the hero of the Willans and Searle books, perhaps—who (whisper it) gives teachers nicknames. "I say, boys," (says our author) "never have anything to do with nick-names. There's nothing manly about that kind of thing." For worse behaviour "the best way would have been to have given himself a good whipping, or have hired the gardener to do it." When he plants a book to fall on a master's head, the saintly Frank arranges for a dictionary to bonk Molesworth instead. When the villain makes a guy in the shape of the headmaster, Fullerton transforms it into an image of Bacchus, to which the boys sing a ditty about the evils of grog before setting the guy on fire. All is soon well, for Fullerton apologises for the falling book, and Molesworth admits his own plan "was a scurvy trick." At the end of the Christmas term the headmaster sends the boys home with a speech, including the homily "They say there are two ends to everything except a pudding and a ring." An American uncle shows up to spend the season with the Fullertons, and ends the book by answering questions with acrostics that spell out the title of the novel. Perhaps that is the very novel on the cover after all, another modernist device. An addendum that lists "books suitable for presents and prizes" includes *The Battery and the Boiler; or, Adventures in the Laying of Submarine Electric Cables* and *The Giant of the North; or, Pokings rounds the Pole;* even more bemusing, *Freaks on the Fells—Why I Did Not Become a Sailor*. Among the books by our present author, I can only speculate about one title—*Will It Lift?* Perhaps it will trouble my sleep.

I'll end with the oddest inscription I have in my collection. It's a 1919 printing of Lewis Carroll's *The Story of Sylvie and Bruno,* inscribed from Daddy to Duncan with many happy returns on May 12th 1919. The verse is in the style of a famed Carroll nonsense poem, which he salvaged from this novel to use in *Alice*. Read comically, the dedication is amusing enough, but at this remove, who knows?

> He thought he saw a new School Boy
> At school in the Old Hall
> He looked again and saw it was
> A penny paper ball!
> Poor thing, said he, poor silly thing,
> It's not my son at all.

Duncan, whoever and wherever you are, I hope you took it in the best spirit.

Sing Your Sadness Deep, Laura Mauro

Daniel Pietersen

LAURA MAURO. *Sing Your Sadness Deep*. Pickering, ON: Undertow Publications, 2019. 236 pp. $17.99 tpb. ISBN 9781988964126.

Horror, I often believe, has to have a sense of place and that sense of place, at least at first, has to feel welcoming. The beckoning lamp in a storm, the town with its manicured lawns. We have to feel at home in a horror story, because if we don't then how can horror do what horror does and turn the comfortable into the uncomfortable? Laura Mauro seems to believe the same thing, but she also understands the need for horror to push boundaries. So she takes us one step further and, more than a simple sense of place, employs a sense of places.

Within this collection we have tales set in quiet corners of America and Britain, Finland and Russia, and then on into the strange places-within-places; London, a world away from the rest of Britain, and the uncannily delineated realms of the marginalized and the migrant. Mauro's great skill is to make readers feel that they know these places until she applies the tiniest pressure and, with the faint crack of something important breaking, we realize that what we thought we knew, thought of as real, was simply an illusion. From the these cracks between expected and revealed reality, Mauro weaves her stories.

In "Obsidian," the cracks appear in the ice on a frozen lake, between the lives of two sisters, across the face of the mirror that separates our world from the world of other beings. The cracks that skitter through "In the City of Bones" spread to the harlequined skin of Anoushka, to the interference-rich shortwave numbers stations that she listens to through the night. "The Pain-Eater's Daughter" feels those cracks as they seep from her father's clients into his own body, as they separate her from her Roma heritage.

Of the thirteen stories in this collection there's no filler or make-weight additions. I could pick any of them to investigate in greater depth for this review, and it would be a story worth talking about. There are, however, a handful that transcend the others by doing something quite beautiful; the stories themselves become cracked, allowing a secret story to emerge.

"Ptichka" ("little bird" in Russian) is perhaps the pinnacle of this brittle layering of cracks. In this story we learn of Marta and her desperation to nurture the new life growing within her. Yet her child, diagnosed with anencephaly while still in the womb, is destined to die and Marta, abandoned by both the man who left her pregnant and a welfare system that has turned its back on immigrants, finds her expected reality cracking into something else. "Ptichka" is a story of hope and loss, and of how sorrow is boiled into madness by the friction between them. Marta's world cracks and, inevitably, she herself cracks along with it. Yet through these cracks floats the vapor of another, more delicate story. "Ptichka," we slowly realize, is a ghost story. More than that, it is a story about the truest of ghosts—the ghosts not of the dead but of the living. It is a story about the ghosts of what we hoped we might become and what we might yet be. Marta's story shows us how innumerable lives have, through no fault of their own, faded into the ghosts who haunt this crumbling mansion of a country. How easily, Mauro reminds us, we too could become those ghosts if the sustenances of life—money, friends, hope—were removed.

Similar threads run through many of the other stories in this collection and, eventually, a remarkable realization occurs in the reader. *Sing Your Sadness Deep* isn't interested in the minor horror of monsters and violence but in something far deeper: the terror of compassion. This is compassion in its truest sense, a near-religious "suffering-alongside," and it's no coincidence that illness, caregivers, and patients appear repeatedly in this collection. Yet Mauro is not interested in the horrified turning away that often accompanies the transformation of wellness into sickness, but rather the captivated terror that comes from suffering-alongside the sick or needy, the taking on of another's sickness. Even "Looking for Laika"—perhaps the longest story in this collection and, with its most immediate narrative concerning the not-weird-at-all fear of nuclear warfare, one that stands slightly apart from the others—maintains a sense of transformative endurance through emotional suffering in the protagonist. The suffering-alongside becomes a suffering-through, a limit experience that creates a new future by cracking open the present. Indeed, few of Mauro's protagonists suffer the most obvious fate of horror stories: death. Rather, they are more often transformed and reborn; strange and unfamiliar, perhaps, but no less alive for it.

All this philosophizing would mean little, however, if the writing weren't up to scratch. Thankfully, it very much is. The reader can open a page at random and find simple, beautiful words. A character is described as "narrow-faced and dark, like a fox in summer colours." Fish swimming through black water become "a strange constellation." Pain made into "writhing matter," "a thick, tumorous mass." Every sentence in this collection clicks into place, delicately crafted to be as precise and meaningful as possible yet never overwritten or heavy-handed, and each of these sentences builds into stories that feel tangible in their reality.

Sing Your Sadness Deep is yet another outstanding publication from Undertow Publications—presented with their now-usual eye for stunning cover artwork and design—and one that showcases a deeply humane writer who delivers powerful, thoughtful work into a genre where suffering is so often dealt out rather than dealt with, where ghosts are unjustly feared rather than loved.

Man as a Mystery

Donald Sidney-Fryer

ARTHUR MACHEN. *Collected Fiction*. Edited by S. T. Joshi. New York: Hippocampus Press, 2019. Volume I: 1888–1895, 546 pp. ISBN 978-1-61498-248-7. Volume II: 1896–1610, 540 pp. ISBN 978-1-61498-249-4. Volume III: 1911–1937, 558 pp. ISBN 978-1-61498-250-0.

MARK VALENTINE and TIMOTHY J. JARVIS, ed. *The Secret Ceremonies: Critical Essays on Arthur Machen*. New York: Hippocampus Press, 2019. 412 pp. ISBN 978-1-61498-245-6.

There can be no doubt that S. T. Joshi has long since become the outstanding scholar of modern imaginative fiction and related materials, the very different kind of fantasy and science fiction, or science fantasy, involving horror and the supernatural, as purveyed by H. P. Lovecraft, Clark Ashton Smith, Algernon Blackwood, and many others, including other British writers, and thus not all associated with *Weird Tales,* the "Unique Magazine" that flourished from 1923 on into 1954, as primarily edited by Farnsworth Wright.

Not only has Joshi, with exemplary care, prepared the corrected texts of any given author, correlating them with first printings and/or with the original manuscripts when and wherever available, but he has also sought out discarded or alternate versions, going far beyond mere professionalism or ordinary devotion to literature. His work is thorough and as impeccable as possible. Joshi himself remains the complete professional and more than that, a creative scholar, a status not at all common or commonplace. Nonetheless, he has his own blind spots, as do all critics and scholars, but he works fantastically well within his limits or limitations. With such an editor we can have complete faith as to the integrity of any given text that he has handled, especially pertinent when it comes to an author as idiosyncratic as Machen.

In assessing the overall register of all that Joshi has edited, we must not overlook the complete collected poetry (including his many translations) by Clark Ashton Smith in three volumes (Hippocampus Press, 2007–08), nor must we overlook the complete collected poetry (including his poetic dramas) by Smith's mentor George Sterling (Hippocampus Press, 2013). And this limited enumeration represents but a fraction of S. T. Joshi's overall labor to date, mirabile dictu!

Joshi's best virtues as a creative scholar are on display in one of the latest and most important productions from Hippocampus Press premiered at the latest Lovecraft gathering in Providence, Rhode Island, the NecronomiCon IV, in August 2019. These are the three volumes of the collected fiction of Arthur Machen. These volumes represent a consummation piously to be wished—and now terminated. All possible kudos to editor S. T. Joshi, the typesetter David E. Schultz, and the owner-editor of Hippocampus, Derrick Hussey—a formidable triumvirate, indeed!

Before we consider the fiction by Machen and the volume of essays on Machen by other writers, let us consider selected aspects of Machen's life as they relate to his oeuvre, no less than something of the background of that life and career. Let us look at the British royal background against which his life played out. Victoria, born in 1819, died in 1901: queen of Great Britain, and sovereign over the entire British Empire, reigned from 1837 to 1901 during a period when that same empire encircled the entire globe and attained its apogée, a period of unparalleled prosperity and social reform for that commonality.

The same dynasty, the House of Windsor, continues to reign since Victoria: Edward VII (1841–1910) reigned 1901–10. George V (1865–1936) reigned 1910–36. George VI (1895–1952) reigned 1936–52. Daughter to George VI, Elizabeth II (born 1926) has reigned since 1952. All during the period from 1819 on into the present a series of remarkable prime ministers have actually ruled, and run the country and the empire.

We mention this royal background for the benefit of the Americans in the U.S., many of whom are not Anglophiles, and who do not know the importance of the British royal family as part of the overall British tradition. The British sovereign, whoever it might be, abides somewhere in the historical or current background. Thus Machen was born in 1863, twenty-six years after Victoria's accession, about one-third through her unparalleled reign, excepting that (so far) of Elizabeth II, who has reigned now sixty-seven years, as compared to Victoria's sixty-four.

Machen was born, educated, and grew up at Caerleon-on-Usk during a very different period from that in which he died in 1947 after World War II. Apparently he was eighteen or so when he emigrated from southeast Wales to try his luck (employment) in the British capital at a time when tradition in various ways probably loomed larger than what it does today. Although he left his hometown, it never left Machen, with all its Roman and Arthurian associations. The Roman ones included not just the very solid Roman walls and other remains of the legionary fortress itself, but also the many items on display in the little Roman museum that contains legionary and other Roman artifacts found in the little town itself and the immediate area.

Sometime before World War I, but obviously after 1912 the following episode took place in Ashton Smith's life as well as in Machen's. As told to the present writer by Genevieve Sully and/or her daughters Helen and Marion, few other Auburnites knew this fact. Somehow a copy of *The Star-Treader* came to the attention of Arthur Machen through the agency of one of Timeus Gaylord's family in England. Machen read it, or at least part of it, and was impressed. The same family member duly reported this favorable reaction back to Smith and his family in California. It must have proven gratifying and encouraging. It also confirmed his mentor Sterling's own high opinion. Collateral approbation from afar is always welcome, especially as emanating from a writer like Machen.

Mark Valentine has argued that Machen, with "The Great God Pan," unintentionally transformed Pan from a "rustic, bucolic image" into one of "illicit sex and cosmopolitan decadence." We cannot avoid contrasting the negative aspects about Pan in the writings by Machen and other English Symbolists with the more positive ones in the writings of the

French Parnassian poets and other writers, which tend to be the radiant and numinous ones of Leconte de Lisle and José-Maria de Heredia. Witness in the latter's unique collection *Les Trophées* the poems devoted to Pan and Priapus. How different is this treatment from that of the English Decadents or Symbolists!—like the difference between day and night!

Finally, but finally, let us now turn our attention to Machen and the works at hand. With the Machen copyrights now legally expired, any enterprising publisher can reprint Machen's texts in any way that he sees fit. Derrick Hussey has taken advantage of this expiration to make available the books on review here, impeccably presented, an overall 1644 pages. Earnest readers and students of Machen receive a great amount of literature for their money. Thus Hippocampus Press has furnished an entire new generation or audience of readers with newly minted materials. This exceptional accomplishment deserves recognition and genuine celebration. For me, especially at eighty-five, reading and rereading these texts has proven an overwhelming experience! I have remained a fervent admirer of Machen and his writings ever since I discovered them as gathered in *Tales of Horror and the Supernatural* (Knopf, 1948). Appositely, this book appeared right after Machen's death.

By the time of my Arthurian research trip with close friend Jack Hesketh (during the early 1970s) in the west and southwest of Great Britain (largely Wales, Somerset, Dorset, Devon, and Cornwall), Jack and I had both become veteran Machenites, and thus we perceived the ever-changing landscape as under Machen's own spiritual sponsorship. Our day-long visit somewhere east or northeast of Caerleon to the Temple of Nodens (a very large temple complex) at Lydney turned into the single most remarkable highlight of our trip in Jack's automobile.

At least one-third or one–half of the fiction collected into the three Hippocampus volumes is completely new to me, above all the short stories, although I recognize "Out of the Picture," "Out of the Earth," and "N," always a special favorite. Here are such memorable works as *The Terror,* "The Great Return," *The Hill of Dreams,* and others, not to mention such unified collections as *The Chronicle of Clemendy* and *The Three Impostors,* as especial in its manner as *The Hill of Dreams*. Altogether then, the set of three volumes represents as rich a feast of unique and erudite fiction as any aficionado could hope to read.

Rather than galloping through all the material new to us for this review, we reserve all this unread stuff to experience at leisure sometime the coming winter of 2019–20. For those readers hungry for intelligent and informed critical commentary on Machen and his literary output, we can surely recommend *The Secret Ceremonies,* as edited by Messieurs Valentine and Jarvis, and as written by some two dozen writers (including Machen himself discussing his own books). In closing these remarks or thoughts on Machen, we would very much enjoy seeing a reprinted and expanded version of Machen's ironic gathering *Precious Balms,* which would include all the reviews of Machen's books (in the British press) as of up to his retirement from writing circa 1937. We would also enjoy seeing his three autobiographical volumes, *Far Off Things, Things Near and Far,* and *The London Adventure,* all gathered into one big tome, and with photos of Machen, his family, and his friends. We must alert the reader that in Volume II, right after *The Hill of Dreams,* he will find Machen's collection of exquisite prose-poems, *Ornaments in Jade.*

Despite all the clever and smart-ass people who pronounced against Machen and his writings during his lifetime, from start to finish, he has indeed survived. These four volumes bear ample witness to that fact of survival. (Oh that marvelous lyrical prose!)

(Clandestine afterthought! Another point of interest between Machen [with his sacramentalism] and the critic redacting this review. Writings about Machen inform us that he was Anglican, High Churchman, Anglo-Catholic. This reviewer was raised as a [Roman] Catholic—a faith long since renounced—but which allows him to understand in depth Machen's own ceremonialism.)

An aside, or postscriptum, please note well. I did not mention in the main body of this review several obvious particulars about Machen and his writing, whether fiction or nonfiction. This non-mention is intentional, and so I shall discuss them here in this concluding aside. Whatever he writes, Machen almost invariably seems discursive, which puts the reader at his ease. This works as an adroit ploy for his fiction. The one exception, or one of the few such, is "The Bowmen," the short story that reads almost like a news report from the battlefield: the miraculous intervention (during World War I) of St. George with his Agincourt Bowmen, or "the Angels of Mons," whereby the English briefly found salvation, and 10,000 German soldiers died. The news media picked this up as something genuine.

Another major point, about Machen's typically indirect mode of narration in his fiction. The narrative itself is clear and suave as the author tells the story, revealing his little surprises as he goes along. In general this functions well for him, if not exemplarily for what it is. Why did Machen adopt or innovate this narrative mode, say, in contradistinction to a bald news report? It creates at once the sense of an interesting and enigmatic puzzle, thus emphasizing one of Machen's major tenets as a "spiritual" writer: that man, or any human being, is a mystery made for mysteries and surrounded by mysteries.

We must add, lest we forget: The covers by Matthew Jaffe and Nicholas Day, and cover designs by Daniel V. Sauer, are both distinctive and original for all four volumes. The frontispiece photos, by E. O. Hoppe and John Gawsworth illustrate and illuminate the physical Machen.

The Unseen, Quiet Dark

Fiona Maeve Geist

MICHAEL KELLY. *All the Things We Never See.* Pickering, ON: Undertow Publications, 2019. 250 pp. $17.99 tpb. ISBN 978-1-988964-14-0.

Michael Kelly occupies the strange position of having been so successful with Undertow Press—publisher of the impeccable *Year's Best Weird Fiction* series and excellent collections by Priya Sharma, Sunny Moraine, and Simon Strantzas, among many others—that it is easy to forget he is an accomplished writer in his own right. *All the Things We Never See* is his third collection and manages to embody the best characteristics of quiet literary horror while always feeling fresh and unsettling with flights of a more postmodern literary bend, such as the metafictional/metatextual "Blink," the occasional poetry—haiku in "Six Haiku" and "Eight Haiku"—sparse yet lyrical prose in "Another Knife-Grey Day" and "A Quiet Axe." There is a staggering variety of unsettling tales relying less on shock and vast cosmic forces to deliver horror. Instead, the stories focus on the cracks in the quotidian, into which dark, bleak, and horrifying things burrow and proliferate.

Take "Tears from an Eyeless Face," which deals with the wish to artistically create while surrounded with the drab trappings of depression. Setting the scene is Kelly's minimalist yet evocative details that capture a totalizing grim haze:

> You've lived in the same small apartment (a tiny, musty box shoe-horned beside other boxes and placed inside a bigger box) in the same grim neighborhood in the same bland city for a very long time. You've walked the same cracked and sorrowful streets, devoid of sunshine and birdsong, shuffling past the same sad citizens—their faces runny grey blurs—for countless years. You shuffle among them, unnoticed, another grey blob on life's large grey canvas.
>
> You've worked the same menial job. You watch endless reruns on the ancient, fuzzy Zenith television. You eat the same

> frozen grey dinner, your mouth like ash.
> Only now, late in your forlorn life, you take an interest in painting. But you discover you have no eyes.

The shattering realization of lacking artistic talent, of being incapable of creating, is effective and cutting given the horrid gray palette with which Kelly paints the tableau. This entwined realization of stultifying numbness and incapability to create explores the various dashed hopes implicit in this rationalization, lending a grim weight to the emotional finale's breakdown: the closing line that "you press your hands to the wall and begin to paint" manages to be subtly cryptic as to the implicit success or failure of the endeavor, creating a certain poignancy. "Other Summers" similarly interrogates how death and promise cut short are everyday tragedies, juxtaposing a carnival and a car-wreck to explore youthful promise and possibilities and pedestrian dreams. The prose itself beautifully captures the sort of wistful sadness trapped inside potential elegantly as the four youths enter the carnival and:

> Still the calliope plays. Light and then dark, soft and then swelling, carried on the night breeze: the music of laughter and dark mystery; of carnivals and funerals; of life and death; of summer itself. Endless summer.
> The sweet summer wind gusts, swirls past them, pricking their skin with gooseflesh, tickling their noses with carnival scents; French fries and ketchup, burgers and coke, peanuts, popcorn, and liquorice. It carries mystery and regret, sorrow and happiness, and all the hopes and dreams of children everywhere. Or so it seems to them, this night, at this moment.

There is a decidedly mournful note to the stories in *All the Things We Never See* that unifies the collection without ever making the stories feel homogeneous; there is enough breadth to the territory explored to keep every story feeling varied while simultaneously belonging together—despite the stylistic range.

Serving this variety exceptionally well is the brevity of the included pieces (rarely exceeding ten pages), yet Kelly utilizes the minimal space effectively—evocative prose without spare lines cluttering the sleek pieces. Among the longest items, "Pieces of Blackness" manages to cover a decaying marriage, difficulty accepting an adopted child, shame and secrets all within eleven pages. The story deftly contrasts more mundane horrors with the sort of general disconnect and disturbance many can relate to. In the former, there is this passage, capturing the tensions rising in the main character Peter's family after adopting a child:

> He stood in a far corner of a barn, smoking. Peter came out here to think. He came out here *not* to think. Katy would be displeased if she caught him smoking. So he kept watch on the barn door. She'd made him quit when they brought Timothy home. She didn't want him to be a bad influence. Peter smirked. Funny, he thought, Katy hadn't once mentioned Peter's health.

The latter involves Peter's adoptive son and Peter finding a jar without breathing holes on Timothy's dresser. Peter remarks, "You can't do that. You can't kill things," and when Timothy inquires why Peter is simply dumbfounded: "He had no good answer for that." These quotidian moments—plaintive, sad, strained, and perplexed—are juxtaposed with the miasmic titular pieces of blackness growing within Peter. Contrast these bluntly stated moments with the feverish climax of the story after "Peter pictured the boy in Katy's bed, tiny mouth sucking at her pale breast. He closed his eyes tight, as if that would shut out the noises. Moisture leaked from the corner of his eyes. He felt close to bursting." Then he heads outside to "Black stars hanging in a cold black sky. A rippling across the dark firmament." The final encounter, built through the accumulation of tiny distressing details, is cryptic; it is simply stated that "The boy was gone. The barn was gone. Katy was gone. There was nothing but the sky, vast and black and unending. Then Peter was gone." An ending that is up to the reader's interpretation, evaluating the details scattered in the text and trying to make sense of them.

Despite the muted nature of the horrific in the various pieces, Kelly delves into unseemly, quotidian, and sorrowful details that give the 'gentler' scares a distressingly powerful punch. *All the Things We Never See* is a dark and hypnotic revelation of a text, slowly pulling readers in and leaving them exposed to the cold, uncaring, indifferent, and inscrutable dark more often than not. This deeply affecting and brilliantly written collection merits a place on the shelf of any contemporary enthusiast for weird fiction. I cannot recommend it highly enough.

Curtains of the Impossible: A Remembrance of Sam Gafford

Farah Rose Smith

I believe it to be the eventuality of most in the throes of loss to hold close their own treasured memories and interactions with those they loved, for internal mourning blossoms and fails to obscure the grief flourishing around us. In the case of Sam Gafford, this is most uniquely true. The days and weeks after his death saw an outpouring of recollections of memories and interactions from those who knew Sam—a testament to the general public how widely loved he was. His influence on so many individuals was significant, and his collective influence on his communities—be they the Lovecraftian, weird fiction, Providence literary scene, or amongst amateur and aspiring writers generally— is what glows most profoundly after his departure. The loss of him is a loss for us all.

Some may know Sam Gafford as the founder of Ulthar Press. Some may know him as a leading authority on William Hope Hodgson and editor of *Sargasso,* an annual journal devoted to Hodgson. Others may know him from his books and magazines, *The House of Nodens, Whitechapel, The Dreamer in Fire,* or *Occult Detective Quarterly,* or perhaps his work with the NecronomiCon convention, to which he dedicated his time and ideas for years. No doubt you have seen him around Providence at reading and events in our community. Without question, many of us know Sam as one of the kindest, warmest, most genuine people we have met not only in the Lovecraftian and weird fiction communities, but anywhere in the world.

In the words of S. J. Bagley, "Sam was one of the warmest, kindest, and wonderful people I have known. He was the heart of NecronomiCon Providence (even when not directly involved) and his loss is immense. We have lost one of the world's foremost experts on both Hodgson and Machen (along with being a fantastic fiction writer in his own right).

But, more importantly, we have lost one of the most inspirationally and contagiously fascinated people that any of us has known. He shared those fascinations with us with such ebullient joy and, by doing so, he truly made the worlds of those that knew him better as he kept the torch alive for weird fiction, comics, and the strange bits in between."

His niece, Madeline Michaud, said, "Though he would never admit it, he was one of those genuine people who was a great friend to many. And when I say that, I mean most of the Lovecraftian and Mythos community."

Author Sam L. Edwards wrote, "Sam was one of the first voices to encourage me when I got here. I often talk about how intimidating it is. Mine wasn't an ease into community. I was dropped off the deep end. Suddenly I was sharing tables of contents with people much more established than me, writers whom I had previously enjoyed as a reader. Throughout all of it, Sam was a pillar. Sam has had, in retrospect, a profound impact on my trajectory as a writer. I am going to miss my friend. But I guess the thing to do is to keep going, live by his example. To be kind and agreeable and encouraging. To try and be the person he would be proud to know."

Derrick Hussey stated, "Everything he wrote, each title he issued, all were plainly the embodiment of Sam's own superb literary and aesthetic vision, ignoring passing fads, always hewing to the highest quality. Everything he did, he did so well. He was the finest imaginable example of a colleague and a friend."

I first met Sam Gafford online, in a Facebook group called the Arkham Horror Book Club. He became such a fixture in my life that I can't recall our first conversations or the first time we met in person. For several years we spoke on Facebook Messenger. In 2016 this changed to emails. Our exchanges were daily, letter-length, and continued on for years and years. We touched upon just about everything imaginable among introverted friends: our love of blues music, during which he told me about his Gretsch guitar that was a "holdover from his rockabilly days," and his old Gibson ES-355 that he sold twenty years ago to pay bills; our love of Elvira, during which he informed me about an old comic based on her that I'd never heard of from consulting his *Overstreet Comic Book Price Guide,* and our plans to try to see her at various conventions that never quite panned out; The Young Adults, a band who were a Rhode Island institution back in the '70s and '80s. He attended almost all their reunions; his dream as a kid to have a full arcade in his basement when I grew up; about being an armchair Ripperologist for nearly forty years; we bonded over Mad Monster Party, Halloween, and the blob-days we would take for ourselves where we'd relax and try to deal with our very similar depressive states. We started a small film society that only met once at The Arcade Providence, where we screened *The Corpse Vanishes* and *The Black Cat,* bonding over our love of old horror films. Most profoundly, he had at various times saved me from taking my own life.

Sam once wrote to me, "I honestly feel that I am one of those old Victorian writers who wrote hundreds of novels only to be completely forgotten except maybe as an answer on *Jeopardy.* I am often reminded of how Lovecraft wrote *The Dream-Quest of Unknown Kadath* and *The Case of Charles Dexter Ward* and essentially just tossed them into a bottom drawer of his desk because he felt that they were so bad that no one would want to read let alone publish them." It is my wish that for Sam's sake, we do not allow this to happen to him or his works.

Sam's revelations during our exchanges were poignant and underlined his wonderful character. It is these beads of wisdom I wish to share with you all, that underline Sam's intrinsic goodness, value as a friend, and advocacy for the introverted, the depressed, and the suffering.

"I often wonder where I came from. Neither of my parents were 'free-thinkers.' I have never been religious and was born too late to be a hippie. Yet I have always lived according to a philosophy of 'live and let live.' I've never passed judgment on anyone (usually saving such judgments to be used against myself) and simply believe that everyone is entitled to live the lives they choose and to be treated equally under the law and by others. I honestly don't care about anyone's sexual orientation, preferring to simply value them according to their own actions and how they treat others. Love, I've always believed, is too precious a thing to subject it to conditions or force it to conform to the standards of others. As you can imagine, this attitude did not make me popular either in school or with my own family. But I remain curious as to how I developed such a mindset when I had grown up surrounded by the complete opposite?"

"I don't consider myself to be very important as a writer, so I never consider myself above anyone else. And I remember what it was like to approach someone who was known and how frightening it was. I may not be the most social of people and have a wide contempt of humanity as a species, but I try to be as friendly and helpful as I can."

"No matter how big or important anyone might feel, there's always going to be someone who has no idea who you are. Just remember that you spoke the truth and, no matter how much others might dislike it, it's still the truth."

"Every relationship is equal parts excitement and terror. Yet we all still try because the alternative is too much to bear."

"It seems to me that every relationship (romantic and friendly) has a certain amount of fear built into it. Certainly, in the beginning of one, fear is strong as there is always that dread that something will happen to ruin it or that a new revelation you make will be met with disgust or, worse yet, change their opinion of you."

"It's not easy, nor does it work every time, but often it's the best way to go because, no matter what, there will always be some people you can't please."

"Just because they may have gotten published more doesn't automatically make them a better person and, if they think that, it's better not to be bothered with them."

"People who are your true friends will know the score and stand by you regardless of what anyone else says. Even if you lose a few 'friends,' you will still have a core group who believe in you and simply wish to see you happy."

Sam Gafford was the ideal friend. A surrogate brother and father to many. A dedicated colleague, loyal and loving husband, brilliant writer and scholar. The loss of him is a hole in the world that will remain evermore, through which my hope is that we continue to sing into, read around, and celebrate. To adapt a quotation of Hodgson to fit the present moment, the last I will say on this page about Sam Gafford is this:

He wrote, and in writing, lifted the Curtains of the Impossible that blind the mind, and looked out into the unknown.

A New Take on the Chambers Mythos

Acep Hale

BRIAN HAUSER. *Memento Mori: The Fathomless Shadows*. Petaluma, CA: Word Horde, 2019. $16.99 tpb. 242 pp. ISBN 978-1-939905-48-2.

I would like to start this review by stating that Word Horde continues to impress with their sense of design. It has long appeared to me that the majority of weird fiction publishers have either opted to publish titles featuring admittedly strong artwork that bears no relationship to the words inside the book or, regrettably, makes no attempt at designing a visually appealing, let alone engaging, cover. In contrast, Word Horde has consistently published books with striking artwork and sharp design that evokes an appropriate mood for the reader from across the room. I would hold them alongside Tartarus Press, which has committed itself to an elegant, unified presentation across its entire line, for truly understanding the proper elements of book design. Whoever is in charge of the art department at Word Horde, I'll gladly buy you a cocktail should our paths ever meet. Book design is a job that seems largely unnoticed and sadly unappreciated, yet what a difference it makes.

Lest *Memento Mori* be judged solely for its cover, I think it's worth taking a moment to appreciate the company it finds itself in as a Word Horde novel. Let's start with *The Fisherman* by John Langan a.k.a. "that book recommended to every new reader in Reddit's r/weirdlit community." *Furnace* by Livia Llewellyn, *She Said Destroy* by Nadia Bulkin, and the collection *Children of the Old Leech* amongst others. Word Horde's editors have had a discerning eye when it comes to their acquisitions. It seems, from an outside perspective, as if they take on only those projects to which they feel they can give their full support and dedication. Therefore, while their catalog is modest compared to some, it is of exceptionally high quality. After this build-up, I am happy to write that *Memento Mori* fits comfortably within this canon.

Memento Mori is the debut novel of Brian Hauser. It takes a montage approach to tell the story of underground filmmaker Tina Mori, her former college roommate, co-conspirator, and future biographer C. C. Waite, Tina Mori enthusiast and fanzine publisher Billie Jacobs, and presumably Hauser himself, or an unknown narrator, as he assembles these disparate fragments into a cohesive whole.

Hauser does not conceal the fact that *Memento Mori* utilizes Robert W. Chambers's mythos. In his novel, the play *The King in Yellow* exists and bears all the properties, and affects its readers, precisely as Chambers describes in the few short stories he wrote on the matter. Hauser uses this as a launching point for his tale of creative obsession, self-manufactured mythologies, the changing nature of friendships, and the ability of art to transform the world.

Hauser obviously loves, and is well versed in, experimental film, and he makes two particularly apt choices in the grounding of Tina and C. C.'s characters. The first is Tina's awakening to cinema via Maya Deren in a beautifully rendered scene that will resonate strongly with anyone lucky enough to have ever spent any length of time in upstate New York; and the second is C. C. Waite's referencing filmmakers from the Cinema of Transgression in her biography of Tina Mori. Maya Deren was an extraordinary visionary who is well worth digging into if you are unaware of her work; it would take far too long to do her justice here (fans of the Lovecraft circle would do well to start with her essay "Amateur versus Professional," originally published in *Movie Makers Annual* 1959). The Cinema of Transgression was a loose group of underground filmmakers from New York City in the early 1980s centered around the director Nick Zedd. This attention to detail, the believability of the timelines involved in the characters' lives, add that extra bit of verisimilitude that assists greatly in the willing suspension of disbelief.

Hauser's love for experimental cinema also shines when he is creating fictive elements wholesale. The description he provides for one of Tina Mori's great lost films, *Imperial Dynasty of America,* reads as if it could have been filmed by The Living Theater in its heyday. A scene he writes that is connected to this film (I do not wish to spoil any of the delights for you), which concerns getting turned around in Lower Manhattan, is so well handled that it simultaneously made me giggle and creeped me out. No Yellow Sign required in those neighborhoods at night, it's still easily possible.

The one qualm I had while reading *Memento Mori* was why does it bother with the King in Yellow mythos in the first place? On the one hand, if readers are not familiar with Chambers's work then it seems as if this is an unnecessary hurdle to overcome, and on the other, if readers are well versed in the mythology, they are forewarned and thus forearmed as to what lies ahead. Given Hauser's obvious skill at weaving his own fantastic and eerie threads, I pondered this for quite some time.

While considering this, my copy of ArcDream's deluxe, hardbound *The King in Yellow* collection with annotations by Kenneth Hite arrived and I determined to read these stories once again to see if I could find a new angle to this question. (In a nice bit of synchronicity, NecronomiCon 2019's ArcDream panel with Kenneth Hite was uploaded to YouTube as I prepared this piece and can be viewed at www.youtube.com/watch?v=40Lk9FbFnCc&feature=youtu.be.) Hite's annotations go beyond the usual mentions of Bierce, Poe, and Stoker and dig into Maupassant's probable influence on the Lethal Chambers (via his short story "L'Endormeuse"), the influence of Baudelaire's *Les Fleurs du mal* on Chambers's description of the King's "tatters" and literally hundreds of other delightful pieces of scholarship. What Hite provides is the knowledge that this is a living mythology. It twists, turns, and adapts as conditions demand. A successful work within this mythology is one in which the mythology adapts and works within a new form and not necessarily one in which the new work is simply a retreading or rehashing of Chambers's own stories. With this being said, the only question was, did *Memento Mori* succeed? I think you already know.

With *Memento Mori* Brian Hauser takes those elements he

knows from being a fan of the subject matter and crafts them into finely honed plothooks. He knows that any cinephiles worth their salt would find the idea of a lost film to be completely enthralling. He knows from studying Chambers's stories that there are devices Chambers utilized in a manner so evocatively that once readers grow aware of exactly what is going on a plot reveal seems secondary. He takes the time to create and craft believable characters we are willing to invest our time and emotions into and then thinks how those characters would react, not only to the situations they find themselves in, but to one another coping with those same events. I believe that Hauser took these ideas and more, thought long and hard about how to best implement them, and only then began writing. That work in laying the foundation pays off many times over.

I feel that parts of *Memento Mori*, the strongest parts in fact, sit comfortably alongside the previously mentioned work, John Langan's *The Fisherman*, in the exploration of friendship and the changes wrought upon friendships by the passage of time and circumstance. There are too many works of weird fiction that concern themselves primarily with the "weird" aspect and sacrifice human elements so that we, the readers, aren't affected by what occurs within the novel. This may be a remnant of Lovecraft's approach to the genre, yet Lovecraft dealt mainly with short fiction. If a writer is to engage the reader's sympathies for the length of a novel concessions need be made. Compelling characters are a sure-fire way to keep a reader's attention. I am not saying a reader must like or empathize with the character, but within the work itself the character must remain logically consistent. Hauser does a remarkable job with this task. While you may not always agree with the decisions his characters make, they ring true unto themselves. This is especially important for a work such as *Memento Mori*, where the novel is dealing with the effects of characters reacting to growing artistic obsession.

Hauser adds to this his own unique take on mysterious collectors and enigmatic groups operating at the fringes of upstate New York and within New York City itself. He utilizes small, elegant flourishes that in their innocence suggest hidden depths, and this quietude is all the more unsettling for its sylvan simplicity. This may be why I found the inclusion of the play *The King in Yellow* so jarring in its forthrightness. While the other elements of the book were being teased in a nicely muted manner, to be bluntly told, "Here's this play, *The King in Yellow* . . . ," seemed a tonal shift that simply felt off.

All this is merely minor quibbling. *Memento Mori* is already on my bookshelf alongside a some of my most often reread and beloved books. It has already earned its spot on the strength of my first reading, and I look forward not only to his future works but to my very next reading of *Memento Mori*.

A favorite from the show, Allan Servoss's "In His House Dreaming," evokes the lurid and lurking depths of the aquatic realms where humans best not tread. ∎

Ars Necronomica 2019: What Drives the Dark Dreams of That Divine City?

Michelle Souliere

Although I am a bookseller by trade, my hidden vocation is art. Because of that, for me the fast-beating heart of the NecronomiCon experience is the art exhibit that parallels the conference: Ars Necronomica. In 2013 and 2015, I was very excited to be a participating artist, and in 2017 and 2019 I played a role both as an artist and as a curator.

In advance of each conference, curators are gathered by some unknown and mysterious star-divined method, charged by director Niels Hobbs with selecting a short list of artists not yet seen in prior incarnations of the show. These curators are sent out into the world at large on a quest. Each must seek out new work evocative of the cosmic horror and weirdness that Lovecraft and his circle of correspondents brought creeping and booming onto this tiny blue planet early in the 1900s.

But what makes art "weird"? What evokes "cosmic horror"? It is difficult to describe that quality in a way that includes/excludes adequately.

In a 2016 email, as we stoked our fires for the 2017 Ars Necronomica show, "Wonders of the Visible Weird," artist and co-curator Gage Prentiss attempted to synthesize his personal concept of that elusive "something" that he looks for when scouting art:

> Draw me in, then overwhelm my senses.
> Show me something that should be safe, but make me doubt that it is.
> Show me a dreamscape I should not tarry in.
> Make me believe in and fear a creature/place/thing that shouldn't exist.
> Convince me of a dark object's provenance.
> Conjure dark, deep places with an ancient presence.
>
> Like all of you, I know it when I see it.

Shown at left are two favorites from the Ars Necronomica 2019 show. *To*p: Bob Eggleton's "Frozen Hell—The Thing," created as cover art for the recently restored edition of "Frozen Hell," the John W. Campbell novella that served as the basis for John Carpenter's *The Thing*. *Bottom*: Kim Parkhurst's "East Side Cultist Riot 1993," a folkloric interpretation of actual occurrences in a tunnel below Providence many wild moons ago. You can find more of her work on Instagram @toadbriar. ∎

Each of the curators has their own ideas for potential talent, formed from our unique viewpoints. Yet somehow as the stars align and the dates for the show come nigh, the process begins to flow more smoothly, and in the end it is reasonably easy for us to reach a consensus allowing for each other's perspectives.

How is this possible? I think, jumping to another literary source for a moment, that Sherlock Holmes said it well: "When you have eliminated all which is impossible, then whatever remains, however improbable, must be the truth." When we compile all the curators' nominees together, we use a ranked choice voting system that, while unwieldy, does indeed cull out work that doesn't speak to that year's particular challenges.

Thus the artistic specimens that display too few of the qualities we envision in the upcoming show are weeded out democratically when a majority of the curators are not able to see that work as part of the intended whole. The results are often surprising, at least in part, but we rarely argue about them. It's a peculiar alchemical process that seems to do the trick and keeps things lively.

The reasons of each curator for inviting their list of new artists are many and varied. Some artists are proposed because a curator likes their non-weird work, and artists are then invited to shift their work toward creating the unthinkable, the indescribable. Some artists are proposed based on their prior known work in the "weird art" field. Others have created pieces that call across language barriers from oceans away, luring a curator to a kindred spirit glowing in the dark far distant. And then there are the surprises that the open call for art brings each time, a summoning that results in an array of work into which the curators determinedly plunge with no protective charms to shield them. Luckily, no eyeballs have been lost (yet).

In the anomalous fashion of all things NecronomiCon, something sets Ars Necronomica apart from any group show I have ever helped curate, a realization that I appreciate most as I walk through the galleries and view this year's wild garden of disturbing enchantments. There is a quality to the Ars Necronomica shows that sets the brain and eye afire alike. It kicks off conversations and responses that sprawl like Nyarlothotep into the future, spawning new and chaotic growth and change in art yet to come.

But what is that quality? There are plenty of other shows that must have a similarly symbiotic and explosive effect on their creative communities, and perhaps it is my poor luck to have not yet encountered them that makes this show seem so unique. I do not know.

It is possible that the fact that Ars Necronomica is run in conjunction with a responsive conference is what makes it so alive. Every time, visual arts in both their current and historic embodiments are incorporated into the panels and talks of the NecronomiCon, as well as being a vital and overwhelming presence in the vendor room.

Another possible contributing factor is that so many artists attend the conference. You will find clusters of us in hotel lobbies and corridors, hobnobbing over sights seen and unseen, and enclaves of us seated in audiences, not only noting down matters spoken of but also intently working on sketches and scribblings that capture the people and ideas presented to us there, or in the audience around us.

It may well be that the vitality of the conference as a whole, and the constant reaching out toward new elements for inclusion, is a spark that makes the conference rife with potential future creativity on every level.

On Sunday, August 20, 2017, a powerhouse panel of young talent gathered in the Biltmore's second-floor Garden Room to hammer out their observations and responses to the topic of "Contemporary Weird Art" in front of a live audience. Present were artists Sara Bardi, Michael Bukowski, Jeanne D'Angelo, Justine Jones, Lee Joyner, Skinner, and Stephen Wilson (according to the program guide, not memory, so please excuse any missed persons). This single talk created a billowing of discussions among my artist friends that roils up in conversations still.

I recently asked Jeanne D'Angelo about her statements during that 2017 panel discussion, and how weird art relates to weird fiction as it is a tension that often fuels her work. She said something that should be glaringly obvious, but which seems to elude many: "I don't think that visual art exists only as a supplement to written weird fiction. It's one of many mediums to express the ideas [of the weird]. [. . .] Many artists are already creating a weird narrative that touches on [. . .] themes and feelings and moods we associate with the genre in the same way an author creates [a weird narrative] with words."

These efforts by creative people everywhere are made public as both personal expression and as an effort of universal communication, to speak of the unspoken, to show a path to the as-yet unseen. I realize that for some people the idea that visual artists as well as literary artists are able to create equally powerful and important work is a given, but for others it is a novel concept.

For some time Jeanne (and others) felt restricted and thwarted by the way in which the weird art directive in particular seemed to overlook pieces that were not directly associated with well-known weird fiction texts, and at the same time found themselves discussing their growing mutual "frustration with the way people disregard the visual art that is connected to the works they enjoy."

Illustration is often seen as secondary and derivative of the texts it depicts. Visual art as a whole, often itself a primary source of inspiration, is likewise well below the public's radar in comparison to the literary art of today. How many contemporary artists can you name as opposed to famous authors?

Jeanne feels that in some ways visual art is even more suited to the purpose of generating new weirdness than the written word: "To me, everything I make has a narrative of its own. I think the flexibility of interpretation that's inherent to [. . .] visual art is *suited to the slipperiness of ideas we tend to class as weird*" [emphasis added].

There was plenty to look at as the show sprawled through two floors of the Providence Art Club on Thomas Street. Clockwise from center: Kelley Hensing's luminous "Portal," Joe Broers "Dunwich County Fair," "Facial Discomfort" by Kali Brown, "Night-Gaunt at Lovecraft's Grave" by Joe Broers, "Cthulhu" by Brett Gray, Caitlin McCormack's delicately disturbing "Overdirt." ∎

In my view, the very flux of these ideas, and their unwillingness to be pinned down, their innate challenge to the viewer and refusal to lie flat on the specimen table and be assigned a category, is part of what makes Ars Necronomica special.

Jeanne also points out, "There's already a long legacy of weird fiction that integrates or revolves around a piece of visual art, [...] or where visual art practice is central to the conversation about creation. Craig Gidney's novel *A Spectral Hue* seems to reflect a bit on this, to give a recent example. Dempow Torishima [author and illustrator of *Sisyphean* and NecronomiCon 2019's guest of honor] shows how an artist can slip between mediums in one work. Clark Ashton Smith also had ideas he chose to express sculpturally or through drawings instead of words."

I believe it is important for us to recall the fact that both literary and visual arts exist in a symbiotic relationship. Each has its own powerful presence, but we are enriched further by their interplay, no matter whether first incited by one or the other. To ignore this is to risk losing access to the rich creative potential this interaction foments. How many pieces in this year's show, conjured out of the deeps of an artist's dreaming brain, will seed the stories of tomorrow's weird fiction in the minds of viewers? It is an endless cycle.

Great work can be driven further when limited by parameters, but one must also take care to foster and not kill development of ideas. Some limitations are too much. When an art show, or on a larger scale an entire convention, is tied so tightly to the work of one author and his peers, one runs the risk of stagnation. From the beginning, Hobbs has been aware of this danger and worked preemptively to forestall this type of decay from occurring.

By urging efforts outward, by accepting challenging art that not only operates outside this traditional range but also creates anew the sense of wonder and trepidation inherent to known work in that range, *one embraces the fear of the unknown*. This presents challenges. There is sometimes pushback, spoken or unspoken, to work that does not relate as directly as some would like to the familiar tropes of Lovecraftiana. Even in a crowd that lauds the fear of the unknown, there is sometimes a blind reaction of resistance to that same unknown. Ironic, no?

Part of the curators' job is that of gatekeepers, but when functioning best the gate swings both ways. While we need to exert some limitations in order to tailor each Ars Necronomica show, or narrow the gap in the gate, we must also let in fresh ideas, embracing the flow of new creative tides by opening the gates to allow these currents in when perceived tradition might dictate otherwise.

Gage Prentiss said it well, back in that same 2016 email: "We want Weird Fiction art in the key of Lovecraft. We want to make a balance. Add some illustrative work from the mythos that would tickle the recognition and nostalgia of the hardcore fan, while posting a clear sign to the uninitiated of where to go if they want to explore the content. The other side is to show some dark weird art that stays away from blatant splatter horror/gothic horror/sexualized horror/tentacles, and settles into a more sweepingly subtle invitation to cosmic horror."

This careful consideration of material is one of the reasons why the Ars Necronomica show will continue to rise back up every two years into our physical realm alive, renewed, and steeped in dark matter to electrify our synapses and the shadows of our souls, as long as we can keep these key philosophies in mind.

For the viewer, Ars Necronomica can delight, disturb, and terrify all at once or one at a time, depending on which artwork you are looking at, and the context in which you discover each piece. The hope is that each time, Ars Necronomica will draw you in, hopefully more than once, to wind your way through the galleries and follow the trail of breadcrumbs between the pieces that really thump you on the head (or turn your brain inside out).

For artists, it is a vast and sometimes dangerously good cornucopia of fuel and challenges. While some of the work, and the ideas discussed with other artists in between scheduled events, can feed the creative mind for all the months of the two intervening years, there are other moments, the dark moments, when it seems as if everything has already been done before and that the individual flame that one has protected and fed for so long is not enough to burn bright and be seen against the myriad points of other galaxies as they wheel above you.

Be brave in the night! The artists who succeed are those who persist in spite of those moments of darkness, and learn to feed that dark matter into the inner fire that forges and creates the next weird image that is entirely your own, no matter how long it takes. There is a great kinship between artists, which I have never felt more strongly than at NecronomiCon, and I promise that we will continue to poke and prod and amuse one another into doing more fascinating work to show at Ars Necronomica and elsewhere.

This is not a treatise. It is an ongoing discussion that will only lie down and die when the last fires of the creative galaxy run out of fuel and vanish in a last gasp of entropy laden dust.

Iä!

NOTE: All photographs © 2019 by Michelle Souliere. To view photos of the Ars Necronomica opening night reception at the Providence Art Club, and the amazing array of the art shown therein, visit www.flickr.com/photos/darkbrilliance/albums/72157710619439748

Facing page: Gage Prentiss's statue portrait of H. P. Lovecraft, with telescope in hand and cats curled around his feet. It stood in an alcove next to the Providence Art Club Entrance, and was the subject of many a selfie throughout the weekend. It was something of a delight to be able to visit with Lovecraft by standing near this life size representation. ∎

Delicate, Collectible Screams

Géza A. G. Reilly

THOMAS LIGOTTI. *A Little White Book of Screams and Whispers*. Baltimore, MD: Borderlands Press, 2019. 132 pp. $30.00 (signed/limited hc). No ISBN.

Thomas Ligotti has been thought of as one of the most enigmatic figures in modern horror. This is a characterization that he himself dismisses in *A Little White Book of Screams and Whispers,* wherein he describes himself as simply someone who does not like crowds. Nevertheless, an interest in Ligotti as a person—most especially his thoughts and opinions on matters outside of his supernatural horror output—has persisted over the years. This interest has spurred the collection of interviews with Ligotti in Matt Cardin's *Born to Fear* (2014), and it is why we have received a second collection of interviews in *A Little White Book of Screams and Whispers*.

I found *Born to Fear* a little repetitive in that the same subjects were brought up in multiple interviews throughout the collection, making the reading a bit tiresome. *A Little White Book,* on the other hand, is diverse in its attention to different subjects (though of course there is some unavoidable repetition throughout, such as the multiple times Ligotti is asked about the relationship between his work and that of H. P. Lovecraft, Emil Cioran, and Bruno Schulz, among other writers). If I had to choose between the two, I would pick *A Little White Book,* having read it twice now without once feeling as though I have read five slight variations in answers to the same question. Perhaps this is also in part due to the shorter length of *A Little White Book,* which comes in at an economical 131 pages.

In these pages, we discover many aspects of Ligotti's history and thought. Much of this is going to be old hat to anyone who has read *Born to Fear* or some of the ancillary criticism written about Ligotti's work, but it is presented here in a way that makes it feel crisp and engaging all over again. That might be due in part to the diversity of interviewers in the collection: Ligotti is interviewed in *A Little White Book* by single individuals, magazines large and small, and, in the latter third of the collection, a variety of Italian and Russian sources. This diversity almost seems to force Ligotti to switch his tone and mood, keeping his answers, even the repetitive ones, fresh and insightful into himself as a person.

Perhaps the best interview in *A Little White Book* is one done for *The Lovecraft eZine,* where selected authors (including Pete Rawlik, John Langan, Joe Pulver, and Salomé Jones, among others) do their best to hit him with provocative questions. Ligotti's answers here are more extensive and professional-sounding than anywhere else in the collection (a fact that he makes note of himself during the interview), and though the lack of a playful spirit that often crops up in his other interviews is notable, it has left abundant ground for interrogation of his thought and experiences. This interview alone, I think, warrants the existence of the collection.

This is not to say that the other interviews in *A Little White Book* are second-rate. All of them are intriguing in their own ways, and the shift in Ligotti's perspectives from 2015 to 2018 (never too far from his ostensible center, of course), and from *Born to Fear,* is interesting to observe. I don't think a single interviewer here really failed to 'get' Ligotti, except perhaps Peter Bebergal of the *New Yorker,* who received some of the only acerbic-seeming responses from Ligotti in the collection. The dedication of the interviewers makes for a refreshing set of content from engaged and mostly thoughtful parties to the figure that has captured their minds and imaginations. Ligotti repeatedly describes the collection of people who have resonance with his thought and opinion as small, but I think that the quality of the vast majority of interviewers suggests precisely the opposite: there are more persons who *want* to hear themselves echoed in Ligotti than he ever expected.

One of the only flaws of *A Little White Book* is the same flaw that I see in much of Ligotti's supernatural horror: it is issued in a collectible edition only. While I understand that exclusivity drives prestige to some extent, it is incredibly frustrating not to have access to an author's work due to limited print runs and exorbitant second-hand market prices for those unable to get in on the first offering. Borderlands Press seems to operate in the collectible edition mold, which means that *A Little White Book,* while reasonably priced, only had an initial print run of 600 copies. As of this writing, the edition is sold out.

Hopefully Borderlands Press will not only bring *A Little White Book* back into print but will also correct the unforgivable number of editorial mistakes that appear here. Ligotti himself is named as the editor on the copyright page; I hope that the publisher will take a second run at completing the job. Almost every interview has internal errors of some kind, ranging from missing words to blatantly incorrect words to spelling mistakes, and in at least one case an interviewer's question was chopped off in the middle. While these editorial mistakes do not harm the thrust of the collection overall, they are more than a little jarring, and thus disappointing.

A Little White Book of Screams and Whispers is a welcome addition to the tradition begun by Matt Cardin's *Born to Fear* (and presaged somewhat by Darrell Schweitzer's analytic collection *The Thomas Ligotti Reader*). Despite its collectability and editorial mishaps, I do think the collection will stand as a fine contribution to Ligotti's corpus. His dislike of crowds and their judgments notwithstanding, I think it is fair to say that the supernatural horror crowd (such as it is) has taken an interest in Ligotti beyond the bounds of his (apparently now defunct) fiction career. Like it or not, the man is interesting to many of us, and *A Little White Book of Screams and Whispers* lets us peek behind the curtain that he has so carefully and deliberately placed around himself. Would that we see more, one day soon.

"When Blue Meets Yellow in the West": *Stranger Things 3*

Hank Wagner and Bev Vincent

For the first two seasons of *Stranger Things,* Hank and Bev discussed the show via email. This year they got together at the Necon writers' conference in Rhode Island (held July 18–21) a mere two weeks after the third season dropped, and chatted about it face to face.

Spoilers Ahead!
It's 1984. For unknown reasons, the Russians have decided it would be a good idea to reopen the "giant cosmic vagina" Eleven so painstakingly sealed at the end of Season 2 (which she accidentally opened in the first place). Having failed in Russia, they infiltrate Hawkins, Indiana (shades of *Red Dawn*), and establish an elaborate base beneath the Starcourt Mall (shades of James Bond, especially of the Roger Moore era), a recent addition to the town that has had a deleterious economic effect on the businesses that previously thrived on Main Street. As the season begins, the Reds have pried the gate open far enough for a stray piece of the Mind Flayer to regain a foothold in the beleaguered town.

Using a science camp project, Dustin Henderson unwittingly intercepts a coded message from the Russians. As a result of the Russians' experiments, the region is experiencing blackouts and Joyce Byers's fridge magnets are losing their magnetism, which sends her down a new rabbit hole, researching the cause. Lingering at the back of her mind is the suspicion that rogue scientists at Hawkins National Laboratory are up to their old tricks. She goads her old friend and potential love interest (and adoptive father of Eleven) Sheriff Hopper into helping her.

For much of *Stranger Things 3,* the action takes place within several small groups, each having its own narrative arc, until all are reunited in the final episodes.

1) **The Scoops Troop** consists of Steve Harrington and Robin Buckley, who work at the ice cream parlor at Starcourt Mall, Dustin and Erica Sinclair, Lucas's smart-mouthed, ice-cream-addicted younger sister. Robin, played by Maya Hawke (daughter of Ethan Hawke and Uma Thurman), is a welcome addition to the cast—smart, savvy, outspoken, and independent, she is the perfect foil for Steve and his shenanigans in trying to pick up women.

Dustin brings his Russian recording to his pal Steve for help, but it is Robin who eventually cracks the code. They enlist Erica, primarily because of her size, to gain access to a guarded storeroom. She's saucy and smart, sarcastically dubbing their plan "Operation Child Endangerment."

Things don't go smoothly for this foursome: they aren't master spies. They end up deep in the bowels of the Russians' secret bunker and spend much of the season trying to escape, while gaining valuable information about its layout.

2) **Hopper and Joyce.** The symbolic father and mother of Hawkins. Chief Hopper is struggling with El's nascent interest in boys, so Joyce counsels him in sensitivity training. Because he knows Joyce is considering leaving Hawkins, Hopper agrees to help her get to the bottom of the latest strangeness in town, as, if she feels safe, she might stay. Their investigation leads to a couple of Russians leaching electricity to power their arcane gadgetry.

Their group expands to four when they capture Alexei, the amiable genius behind the Russians' experiments, necessitating a visit to Murray Bauman, the only readily available person who speaks Russian. After being plied with junk food and American cartoons, Alexei fills Hopper and Joyce in on what is happening beneath their town. Hopper wants to go straight to Starcourt, but Joyce wants to make sure her kids are safe first.

3) **Mike & Eleven; Max & Lucas; Will.** Teenage love is in the air for the couples. Lucas and Max have been going out for a while, but it's all new for Mike and El. They have no idea how to negotiate the complicated world of relationships. Hopper, upset at his little girl showing signs of growing up, doesn't help when he puts the fear of God into Mike to cool things down a bit. His actions cause a temporary rift that inspires El to seek

advice from Max. The two become gal pals, something El has never experienced before. Since they're teenagers in a small town, this means the ladies make an obligatory sojourn to the mall, the secret epicenter of the Russians' operation.

Much of the season's humor comes from Lucas's attempts to coach Mike on how to repair his broken relationship, even as he stumbles through his own. Will is very much the fifth wheel in this group, growing progressively more frustrated. He also serves as an early warning system of sorts, since he is still connected to the Mind Flayer in ways no one fully understands.

4) **Nancy and Jonathan.** Their relationship has grown more serious, to the point where Nancy is sleeping over at his place. She thinks they're doing it surreptitiously, but Joyce is well aware, and indeed approves, of what's going on, even as Nancy slinks out a window in the morning. The pair now works at the *Hawkins Post*, Jonathan as a photographer (legions of young fans wondered what he was doing in the mysterious "red room" where he was developing film) and Nancy as an errand girl who wants to become a full-fledged reporter, à la Nancy Drew. They encounter their piece of the puzzle when Nancy defies orders and investigates a report from an elderly woman complaining of rabid rats in her basement and missing fertilizer. She intuitively knows there's a big story here, but the old boys' club back at the *Post* (their ringleader is played by a decidedly unenlightened Jake Busey) pokes fun at her and treats her like a joke. Think of the duo as Hawkins' version of the intrepid Karl Kolchak, fighting to expose what's *really* going on.

The Big Bads come in a variety of shapes and sizes. There's corrupt Mayor Kline, who has been badgering Hawkins residents into selling their property to the Russians for his own benefit. There's the relentless Terminator (Grigori) and the other Russians trying to put the genie back into the bottle after Hopper and Joyce capture Alexei. Max's older brother, Billy, has been conscripted by the Mind Flayer as a minion and is building a small army of "flayed" Hawkins residents. And, finally, of course, there's the (mini) Mind Flayer itself, building a monster out of the liquefied remains of these residents so it can confront its nemesis: El, doing her best *Dark Phoenix* imitation, gesturing to ward off the forces of evil.

Bev: *Stranger Things* has become a cultural phenomenon and a huge success for Netflix. Over 18 million people watched the entirety of Season 3 within the first four days after its July 4 global launch, and at least twice that number had at least started watching by then, more than any other film or series on the streaming platform.

We could spend this entire essay pointing out the myriad homages and cinematic references—*Back to the Future* is a big one—from the 1980s (those suffering ST OCD can Google the *New York Times* article that avidly laid out most of them). One key theme, though, is about the shopping mall causing the death of the small town, with its obligatory sleazy mayor leading the charge.

Hank: Cary Elwes, channeling the mayor from *Jaws* and Gene Hackman in *Superman*. Seriously, how many ways can Hawkins die? It was already on the skids, due to natural and supernatural causes. The mall accelerates its demise. People have left Hawkins because there's nothing for them there anymore. Not because of the creepy stuff, which few are aware of; most have just left for greener pastures.

Elwes was just one great part of a stellar ensemble. One of the really cool things about Season 3 was that no actor was wasted. Everyone had a meaningful part to play, and everyone hit their marks.

Bev: Everyone got important things to do—amazing, considering the size of the cast.

Hank: For instance, Scott Clarke (Randy Havens) had only a few minutes on screen, but managed to stand out nonetheless. Murray Bauman (Brett Gelman, now seen in Season 3 of *Mr. Mercedes*) was also great. Dr. Alexei (Alec Utgoff), the Russian scientist, a.k.a. Smirnoff, was terrific, even though he couldn't speak English. Basically, anybody who turned up did themselves proud. Doris Driscoll (Peggy Miley), the little old lady with freaky rats in her basement, stole every scene she was in. Grigori (Andrey Ivchenko), the Russian enforcer, obviously a homage to the Terminator (who also gave off a Rondo Hatton vibe), provided a credible human menace.

Bev: Everyone took control of his or her own destiny. When Hopper tells Joyce "this is a two-person operation" (excluding her), she and Murray come up with a new plan that includes her. There were two times when Joyce seized the reins, dressing people down when they stood in her way: Murray, when he's being precious about bringing a Russian into his secret lair, and the phone call with the FBI contact. She is a fierce protector of her kids.

Hank: And also the town in general. Hopper's the go-to guy. Joyce is the mother of the town, and he's the father. Maybe we laugh at Dad when he's wearing his Hawaiian shirt and black socks, sitting there with a beer in his hand and falling asleep in front of the TV, but when the chips are down we seek him out. He gets the job done. It isn't always the cleanest, neatest thing. He also has a sense of humor about it, bravely showing his "dad bod." We know that Hopper can take a punch now, too.

Bev: I liked the scene where he let Alexei go. He had absolute faith that he knew how this guy was going to react. He's been doing this all his life. We also learned that Steve can win a fight, much to everyone's surprise.

Hank: I was so charmed that Steve and Dustin were so glad to see each other.

Bev: They're a most unlikely duo.

Hank: Steve has the best overall series arc.

Bev: He does. At the end of the first season, when he shows up with Nancy, everyone was upset that she picked the wrong guy. And maybe she did, but he proved to be a much better guy than we thought back then.

Hank: He's so clueless, but he's getting a little smarter. He's got an innate, instinctive intelligence.

Bev: But not enough to get him into community college.

Hank: He probably could. It's probably just a confidence thing.

Bev: He took Robin's "revelation" well. Stunned silence for a few seconds as he processes her news, and then accepting her as a friend, instead of a love interest, in much the same way that El and Max became friends. I noticed that everybody got to be a hero at least once this season.

Hank: All the kids are so used to that. They acknowledge that they live in a weird world, like the Scooby Gang in *Buffy the Vampire Slayer*. They almost go dormant when things are calm, but then they're ready to go at a moment's notice when trouble comes.

Bev: Murray shows up with Alexei's plans proclaiming where everything is and what they have to do, and Erica spouts out that if they followed the adults' plans, everyone is going to die.

Hank: Murray's main skill is in instinctively knowing who is in love by the way they were arguing, something he's shown twice now.

Bev: He's one of those characters who crept into the series and became part of it. Max is another, introduced in Season 2, and now fits well into the group. She has some great scenes when they suspect her brother might be the bad guy. He's never been very good, but she desperately hopes he isn't as bad as they think.

Hank: I think the show runners know how to work their cast now. When they add somebody, they become an integral part of the team, the world. They're having a ball, I think. They're having fun. They work to the strength of the kids' characters and their native intelligence. They don't fold up when bad shit happens.

Jonathan's another go-to guy. I liked that Nancy and Jonathan had their big blowout and then apologized.

Bev: All the couples had that moment. Mike and El have their breakup. Max and Lucas were always at each other's throats.

Hank: You have to work through it. They're becoming adults.

Bev: Except for Will, who, through the first several episodes, only wants to play D&D. He doesn't want anything to change. He's got no use for all that girl stuff yet. He's lagging behind the others in that regard.

Hank: The other guys are trying to figure out what women are.

Bev: A different species. Will did get his end-of-childhood moment eventually. Once he figured out the Mind Flayer was back, everything else went into the back seat. Even D&D.

I liked the discussion about being a nerd. Erica thought she was insulting the older kids by calling them nerds—she can't believe her brother had anything to do with previous brave adventures—but Dustin embraced the label and challenged her on that with his scientific proof, the "My Pretty Pony" discussion.

Big question: New Coke or Classic? Where do you stand on that? The original *The Thing* or the remake?

Hank: Do you try to do homage or come up with your own stuff? Do you just make it slightly different and then it's okay? It goes back to Neil Gaiman and his concept of the storytelling "stew." You take something out, then you put something back in.

Bev: One thing they've done in every season is splinter the group into different subsets that have individual adventures—the Scoop Troop, the nerds, the Griswalds—before bringing them all back together.

Hank: Because they're stronger together. They're a big, extended family.

Bev: This isn't their first rodeo; they've been through this before. When they step up, we know they've got what it takes. There's no dithering. They come up with whatever weapons are at hand and defend themselves—and one another. They know how to face these situations.

Hank: Speaking of family, we haven't discussed the fact that they've pretty much ignored the fact that Eleven had "sisters." She had her moment of growing up in Season 2 and then she sort of regressed, and it's all over a boy? Everything else had a callback. They nodded to all the supporting characters again.

Bev: I wasn't sorry that they didn't bring that external mythos back in this season. It was my least favorite part of the second season.

Hank: Even if Hopper had said something like, you know, when you came back from Chicago, you were different . . . kind of a nod that it happened. And she went to Chicago but doesn't know what Illinois is? That's another thing that bothered me.

Bev: And she'd never been to a mall before.

Hank: But she's been on a heist!

Bev: They had to keep reminding us of the things she knew or had experienced and those she hadn't.
    My favorite part of the third season was exploring a woman's right to determine things for herself. Men trying to do things for women and the women coming back with, thanks for the help, but we've got this. We have a plan, too, another way of doing things. It starts with Mike's jealousy, because El was spending time with Max. It develops into his concern that she's taking on too much and she's going to hurt herself. Max reminds him that she's her own person, she knows what she can do better than anyone else and, by the way, she's saved the world twice already.

Hank: I liked the women's empowerment, but it was still the '80s so they weren't fully vested. ERA was still being talked about, and states were voting against it.

Bev: Nancy had her moment with her mother, after she got fired. Her mother's explanation of what life was like for women at that time.

Hank: They played with the music a little bit. They weren't strictly '80s. The Cars were popular then, but debuted in the late '70s. I loved that they used *American Pie,* fading out as it played in one of the middle episodes.

Bev: I thought sometimes the choice of music was just a little bit too on the nose.

Hank: Too precious.

Bev: They picked the lyrics very carefully to match what was going on.

Hank: My biggest complaint about the show was Billy's mustache. I just hated that, wanted to shave it the heck off. And maybe trim that mullet. But Billy also had quite an arc, moving from general bad boy to Big Bad and . . . well, let's not spoil EVERY surprise.

He reminded me of Randall Flagg. That whole idea of him on the highway and suddenly he's able to do magic? That was Billy, at first shaken, then growing used to the idea of being possessed.

Also, we should have a drinking game based on how many times people were thrown into walls this season. Maybe there's a metaphor there? And another drinking game for every time Eleven does her power gesture, resulting in a nosebleed?

Bev: Why did the Russians want to open the doorway? They never answered that. We don't even know how they found out about the Upside Down in the first place.

Hank: It could be just like the race for the nuclear bomb—everyone working toward the same goal, in different places. Or it could be because of spycraft/counter-intelligence work.

Bev: I have two criticisms of this season: the "show-stopper" in the final episode; *The Neverending Story* duet. Dead stop. A full 60 seconds.

Hank: It would have been nice if they'd done a few seconds and then had Dustin get so embarrassed that he called it off. But he loves Suzy.

Bev: It went on far too long. And I thought they overdid the "match cuts," where the scene shifts to another shot that's similar, but different. There's something swirling at the end of a scene and then you jump to a toilet bowl flushing in the next. Once or twice that's clever, but after a while it got to be too much.

Hank: The effects were state-of-the-art, but, appropriately, they looked a little '80s and cheesy, too. They were very overt with the horror this season, as when people were decomposing, and exploding. But they prepared you well with the exploding rats.

Bev: There were a lot of scenes where someone showed up at exactly the right moment to save a situation.

Hank: It *is* a small town. But there were enough moments when nobody showed up, too.

Bev: Yeah, you really felt everyone was in genuine peril. It never felt as if they were holding back. Anybody could potentially go.

Hank: I wonder what they're going to parody or homage next. Are they going to do Chernobyl? That's really where I thought they were headed this time. All the kids are going to be grown up in Season 4. They're all going to be driving, college-bound.

So, in the end, we both give Season 3 an enthusiastic thumbs up. Good, linear storytelling. It sped along.

Bev: Absolutely. I had no trouble watching the whole thing a second time almost immediately. I'm anxious to see Season 4.

Hank: As am I.

Train Reading

Peter Cannon

On the train ride from New York to Providence, one of the two books I brought with me to read was *Moby-Dick*. I first read Melville's masterpiece when I was sixteen. I reread it twice over the next few years. Decades later, I decided to read it a fourth time for two reasons: 2019 was the bicentennial of Melville's birth, and I had recently learned from the Lovecraft letters to J. Vernon Shea that HPL had read *Moby-Dick,* something that I wasn't sure of when I wrote "Call Me Wilbur Whateley: Echoes of *Moby-Dick* in 'The Dunwich Horror,'" an essay first published in *Crypt of Cthulhu* in 1987. Indeed, Lovecraft, whose copy of *Moby-Dick* surfaced in 2015 among the collection of the American Antiquarian Society, uses the word *cosmic* in urging Shea to read it. Imagine my surprise and delight, then, when I came across certain evocative phrases in the chapter entitled "The Whiteness of the Whale": "vague, nameless horror"; "a certain nameless terror"; "the nameless things of which the mystic sign gives forth such hints"; and "the invisible spheres." The Old Gent must have smiled at language so similar to his own.

The other book was John Connolly's *A Game of Ghosts,* the fifteenth entry in the author's supernatural detective series, which I had known for a while reflected a Lovecraft influence but only now decided to sample. In the first chapter, private investigator Charlie Parker, the series hero, meets someone at a diner in Portland, Maine. Charlie has a "general distaste for shellfish and seafood." The action eventually moves to Providence, R.I., where, as I later learned on the train back to New York, Charlie goes to a place to eat in the Arcade opposite "a store called Lovecraft Arts & Sciences."

During the convention, I was on several panels. Since I often felt I had little to say on the nominal topics, I digressed whenever I could on the Melville influence on Lovecraft and the Lovecraft influence on Connolly. At the end of the panel on HPL and the Gothic tradition, someone in the audience asked whether Melville's story "The Piazza" influenced "The Strange High House in the Mist." I was stumped, but fortunately another panelist, a young academic better versed than I in Melville, had some sort of an answer.

I also made a point of mentioning Adrian McKinty's recently published *The Chain*, a bestselling thriller set in Massachusetts that I read soon after hearing from the freelancer who reviewed it for *Publishers Weekly* that it contained Lovecraft references. In an early chapter, the heroine, who lives on Plum Island, visits the Newburyport Public Library, where she "finds an empty study cubicle in the Lovecraft wing." In a late chapter, the heroine receives instructions to go to a restaurant at Logan Airport and "order two Cthulhu ales and two chowders." The climax takes place in the Miskatonic Valley.

The Chain, to the author's credit, also alludes to Orwell, Snoopy, James Bond, and prime numbers. I highly recommend it apart from the nods to Lovecraft.

My NecronomiCon 2019: Wanderings and Wonders

Elena Tchougounova-Paulson

Joyce Carol Oates once said: "Everyone has at least one story to tell. . . . You should be writing about things that surprise you." I wish I could have the talent and stamina (also, a richer English vocabulary) to describe my wanderings and wonders around NecronomiCon 2019 properly.

To put it straight: I was waiting for this event since my first experience back in 2017, and I was as desperate, and impatient, and anxious as Vladimir and Estragon together. My very first NecronomiCon was absolutely fabulous: I met my fellow Lovecraftian people; I participated in the Armitage Symposium (many thanks to honorable Professor Dennis Quinn); I saw all the locations linked to the Old Gent with my very eyes. That being said, my first NecronomiCon left me craving more, and I was very much looking forward to doing it again.

And so it went, and it happened: this time I arrived to Boston (Arkham in an alternative universe) and came to Providence in the late evening of Thursday. To my surprise, I did indeed remember all my routes and paths, and found the opulent Omni without any trouble (knowing me and my topographical awkwardness—let us put it this way—I must admit that was a striking achievement).

Providence was splendid. Providence had remained exactly as when I left it two years ago. And then the unexpected occurred. To my horror, at the registration desk for NecronomiCon 2019 I found out that I had forgotten to register for a walking tour around the Lovecraftian locations! I still have no clue how it happened (N.B.: Please, never be sure until the end that you are safe with all your preparations! Check yourself as many times as you can!), and it was certainly heartbreaking at first, but the level of support I got from my friends and colleagues in regard to my silly misfortune was overwhelming: people gave me advice on how to do it in the most reliable way, and it did work in the end.

I managed to visit all the sacred (for devoted HPL fans) places, starting with Downtown (Biltmore/Graduate, Lovecraft Arts & Sciences, Fleur-de-Lys Studio etc.) and College Hill (Brown University with its Van Wickle Gates, John Hay Library, Athenaeum, H. P. Lovecraft Memorial Square, 10 Barnes Street, Samuel B. Mumford House [65 Prospect Street], etc.) and ending my tour in Swan Point Cemetery, by Lovecraft's grave.

And, of course, the Armitage Symposium! Needless to say, that it was glorious. This time I was involved in quite a few panels and talks: I gave my own presentation in the "Literary and Philosophical Studies" panel, and also was a moderator of a panel, "Lovecraft, Science, and the Environment." Apart from the fact that all these talks were incredible and all the participants did fantastic research, I have to admit that I profoundly hate to interrupt presenters and remind them to stick to the schedule: I wish we had twice as much time! But tempus fugit, phew!

Perhaps my most memorable experience was connected with my involvement in two other discussion panels: "Sacred Objects, Sacred Places: The Importance of Shrines, Idols, and Religious Artefacts in HPL," in which colleagues and I discussed why the sacred was so important to Lovecraft despite his firmly committed atheism, and "Welcome to Weird: A Beginner's Guide to Weird Fiction," in which the panel tried to provide our own definitions of the genre. I must admit, when I faced the vast audience at the former ballroom, I was freaking out a bit, thinking: "What if I fail and all my monologues turn into complete gobbledygook?" But the atmosphere there was so friendly and warm, that all my fears (mental night-gaunts, right?) disappeared to my great relief.

The only problem was that everything good has a tendency to end too quickly, and that was what exactly happened to NecronomiCon. It was over, but somehow in my mind I am still there, and I want to go back. In two years. I do hope so.

The Rocky Beginnings of *Weird Tales*

Darrell Schweitzer

JOHN LOCKE. *The Thing's Incredible! The Secret Origins of Weird Tales.* Elkhorn CA: Off-Trail Publications, 2018. 299 pp. $35.00 hc. ISBN 978-1-935031-25-3. $20.00 tpb. ISBN 978-1-935031-24-6.

The Thing's Incredible! is a significant piece of scholarship, filled with new insights and information. It is unreservedly recommended. While I do not think it will upend our understanding of where *Weird Tales* magazine came from and why it is important, it certainly does add much detail.

It is probably best read alongside a set of the Girasol Collectables facsimiles of the early *Weird Tales*. Those are themselves out of print and appreciating rapidly in value (about $100 each in recent eBay listings), but for a brief, shining moment it was possible to read the otherwise virtually unobtainable 1923–24 issues without spending thousands of dollars apiece on them. To do so is a revelation, mostly of precisely how rocky the beginnings of *WT* really were. *WT* may be remembered today as the greatest of all fantasy pulps, and one of the most famous of all pulp titles of any sort, but it was decidedly *not* a great magazine at the outset. One of the things you appreciate in such context is that *any* story by H. P. Lovecraft, even the most minor (e.g., "The White Ape," a.k.a. "Arthur Jermyn") must have seemed like a work of flaming genius compared to what was printed alongside it, and when "The Rats in the Walls," arguably the strongest American horror story since Poe, appeared in the March 1924 issue, it must have seemed like a miraculous bolt of lightning from a clear blue sky.

To be fair, *WT* of this period is best described as a junk bag with occasional gems in with the dross. It was a profoundly ugly magazine, very badly designed, with poor covers that rarely reflected the contents. They probably did not display well on the newsstands. In an era in which pulp magazines sold on the basis of bright, colorful covers, the fledgling *WT* had dull, badly drawn covers, often in two colors or monochrome. It was a cheap magazine, in appearance and content, for the most part written by newcomers and amateurs, since it paid poorly, and was generally viewed as "down market" by professional pulp writers. But this became part of its legacy. Even in its glory days, to the sort of hack who judged success purely on the amount of money made, and who would move from weird fiction to westerns to detective stories to whatever else paid the highest rates (for many, in the 1930s, that meant the *Spicy* line), *WT* was very much a junior publication, something one "graduated from" when one really mastered the pulp trade. (E. Hoffmann Price, despite a certain nostalgia for the old days, consistently displayed this attitude in his memoirs.) The result was that it became a magazine for artistic writers like Lovecraft or Clark Ashton Smith, who were not so much concerned with climbing the pulp ladder of success as *actually interested in writing fantasy,* and would do so for the only market available, regardless of what it paid.

Locke shows us why that market was so marginal. *WT* began as the brainchild of one Jacob C. Henneberger. The first big revelation is that there was a co-founder, John M. Lansinger, who has until now largely been edited out of the story. Henneberger and Lansinger were old pals from youth, and one of the costs of the breakup and reorganization of Rural Publishing Corporation was the end of their friendship. Another revelation is precisely how unsuited the first editor of *WT,* Edwin Baird, was for the job. Baird was something of a wildman, capable of complaining in the most condescending terms about the quality of the slushpile submissions he had to endure, both in his own editorials and in articles for writing magazines. (The title of this book comes from a piece in *Story World and Photodramatist,* October 1923: "The thing's incredible! Manuscripts improperly punctuated, manuscripts with misspelled words and ludicrous blunders of grammar; manuscripts with muddled plots, impossible plots, no plots . . .") At some point Baird may have just cracked, or decided to stick it to Henneberger, because he deliberately published—as a serial no less—"The Transparent Ghost," the worst manuscript he could find, as if to say, "Look! This is what I have to put up with!" It was as if the editor of the *Magazine of Fantasy & Science Fiction* suddenly lost his marbles and published that legendary classic of awfulness, Jim Theiss's "The Eye of Argon," in *F&SF's* venerable pages. Needless to say, a magazine so edited could not last long, and it didn't, scarcely more than a year before it was many thousands of dollars in debt and headed straight over a cliff.

The result was a spectacular blowup. Someone (probably Otis Adelbert Kline) edited the enormous anniversary issue (May–June–July 1924), and then a "reorganization" took place. At one point Farnsworth Wright, who had been an editorial assistant all along and may actually have replaced Baird much earlier than is commonly believed, resigned and published a letter in a writers' magazine stating that he had nothing whatever to do with *WT*. This may have been a dispute over Henneberger's failure to pay his writers. But he and Henneberger must have become reconciled, and, as Locke suggests, agreed as gentlemen never to speak of the matter again, because they didn't. By late 1924, Wright was firmly in charge as editor. Henneberger and Lansinger had parted company. Baird was left as editor of a companion magazine, *Real Detective Tales,* for which he was probably more suited. Lansinger had also walked off with Henneberger's other brainchild and cash-cow, *College Humor,* which was a major cultural institution at the time. Henneberger fades from the scene, with much of the *WT* stock owned by a Mr. Cornelius, the printer. Farnsworth Wright then began the magazine's slow, painful crawl upward into excellence.

It was during the first year and a half of the magazine's existence that Henneberger, desperate for any competent contributors, was aggressively cultivating H. P. Lovecraft, not merely as his star author but as a ghost, intended to write a series of "true" stories for the magician Harry Houdini, who was featured very prominently on a couple of covers. (The only Lovecraft–Houdini "collaboration" was of course "Imprisoned with the Pharaohs," the cover story on the anniversary issue.)

More than that, Henneberger dangled a series of carrots in front of Lovecraft, who (wisely) did not take them entirely seriously. Henneberger offered Lovecraft the editorship of (HPL's phrase) "a brand new magazine to cover the field of Poe-Machen shudders." Did this mean an entirely separate, more highbrow publication, or a revamped *WT*? The job would have involved a move to Chicago. It was not just Lovecraft's obsessive refusal to leave New England (or at least the East Coast, since he was living in New York at the time) but probably good sense that caused him to turn the Henneberger down. Given the extreme instability of the whole operation, HPL could well have found himself a couple months later unemployed and stranded in an uncongenial city. Ultimately Henneberger proposed to start another humor magazine, to rival the one Lansinger has taken away from him. He hinted that Lovecraft might possibly edit it, and first asked him to work up some jokes.... A less appropriate assignment for Lovecraft would have been hard to imagine. ("So two shoggoths and a ghoul shamble into a bar ...")

Locke admits, and I think he is correct, that Farnsworth Wright was a far more suitable choice for the editorship of *WT* (or any proposed new magazine) than Lovecraft, because Wright had, at least, some business experience and, more importantly, knew how to balance art and commerce in a way Lovecraft never could. If Wright erred, it was on the side of caution. He was notorious for rejecting the best and most ambitious stories from Lovecraft, Clark Ashton Smith, et al., largely because he was afraid the readers would not understand them. Having been through that very rough patch in 1924, Wright knew what failure meant. The magazine's survival was always precarious, even in its best years. If he rejected *At the Mountains of Madness* and "The Shadow over Innsmouth," it is worth remembering that only Wright, of any editor in the English-speaking world, could or would have possibly published "The Outsider" or much of the work of Clark Ashton Smith. It was always a delicate tradeoff.

There are only a few places where I think Locke misses the point. He doesn't see C. M. Eddy's infamous necrophilia tale "The Loved Dead" (as revised by HPL) as funny. I seem to recall reading a description of Lovecraft chuckling aloud as he larded on the purple prose. The ending, in which the promising young ghoul slashes his wrists while sitting on a gravestone, bleeding to death as he *still writes in his diary,* is hardly likely to strike most people as "elegant," contrary to Locke. No, it is self-parody, on the order of "The Hound."

The suggestion that Otis Kline and Farnsworth Wright himself were lifting ideas from Lovecraft for their stories seems to me to be quite a stretch.

But, quibbles aside, this is an excellent book. One might fault it for an excess of background detail in some places, e.g., about the early lives and careers of figures only tangentially connected to the main story, such as Otis Kline or Arthur J. Burks, but one is also sympathetic with the researcher's desire to preserve hitherto unknown facts once they have been discovered. We are given several appendices, including one of Baird's rants, an article on writing fantastic fiction by Kline (which is mostly about his own work), a letter from Henry S. Whitehead decrying the general editorial prejudice against fantasy, a witty bit of doggerel by Wright about the editor's plight, and even a story by Wright (from the *Overland Monthly,* 1919) which is of autobiographical significance. You read it all here first. You won't find it anywhere else.

Sam Gafford and Ulthar Press

S. T. Joshi

FARAH ROSE SMITH, ed. *Machinations and Mesmerism: Tales Inspired by E. T. A. Hoffmann.* Warren, RI: Ulthar Press, 2019. 262 pp. $24.95 tpb.

I first came in touch with Sam Gafford (1962–2019) no later than 1981, and when he first visited me in 1982 I was a graduate student at Brown University and was happy to show him around the Lovecraft sites in Providence, R.I. At that time Sam was a great devotee of Lovecraft, but his interests rapidly expanded to both classic and contemporary weird fiction. For some years he appeared to be merely an enthusiastic fan, and his early writings were relatively crude and immature. But then he surprised me when he submitted a superb essay, "'The Shadow over Innsmouth': Lovecraft's Melting Pot," which I was published in *Lovecraft Studies* for Spring 1991. Sam and I collaborated on a review of Stephen King's *Four Past Midnight* and Peter Straub's *Houses without Doors* (*Studies in Weird Fiction,* Spring 1991), Sam covering the King book and I covering the Straub.

Sam, noticing that the field of Lovecraft studies was being well covered by an array of scholars and critics, decided to focus on an author who was then receiving much less attention: William Hope Hodgson. Through diligence and tenacity, Sam eventually became the leading authority on Hodgson. His pioneering essay, "Writing Backwards: The Novels of William Hope Hodgson" (*Studies in Weird Fiction*, Spring 1992), came to the incredible conclusion (based on consultation of some of Hodgson's letters) that the massive novel *The Night Land* (1912) was in fact the first novel Hodgson completed; not surprisingly, he was unable to find a publisher for this heroic tome at the time, and so he turned to writing shorter novels that had greater popular appeal. Sam's *Hodgson: A Collection of Essays* (Ulthar Press, 2013), slim as it is, contains a sheaf of solid research on the British writer. Sam also edited three issues of a fine journal devoted to the author, *Sargasso* (2014–16), and collaborated with Mike Ashley and myself in assembling a comprehensive bibliography of Hodgson, included in *William Hope Hodgson: Voices from the Borderland* (Hippocampus Press, 2014), edited by Massimo Berruti, Sam, and myself.

By this time Sam had, much to my own surprise, become a fiction writer of substantial talent. When I began soliciting stories for my first *Black Wings* anthology, around 2008, Sam sent in the poignant tale "Passing Spirits," a haunting narrative in which Lovecraft figures as a character (of sorts). I regard it as one of the three or four top-tier stories in the book. I published several other stories by Sam in other anthologies and was happy to help him assemble his first (and only) story collection, *The Dreamer in Fire and Other Stories* (Hippocampus Press, 2017).

Even more to my surprise, Sam expanded his range into the novel, writing the superlative Lovecraftian tale *The House of Nodens* (Dark Regions Press, 2017). But he excelled his own high standard with *Whitechapel* (Ulthar Press, 2017), an immense but utterly riveting novel about Jack the Ripper, with the young Arthur Machen as a kind of detective figure. The size of this book compelled Sam to publish it himself, but in this case that is no sign of inferiority. It is, in fact, one of most scintillating weird novels of recent years, fusing a deep knowledge of Ripper lore (of which Sam was a noted authority) with an equally deep knowledge of the London of the period and of the life and work of Machen. It deserves the widest possible readership.

In the course of his career Sam established two micropresses. The first, Hobgoblin Press, published several works by Hodgson, Machen, and other classic authors in the 1990s. The books were somewhat primitive in design, but still managed to get some rare and valuable material back into print. More impressively, Sam's recent imprint, Ulthar Press, has done landmark work in disseminating scholarship on Hodgson, but has also promoted the work of longtime fantasy artist Jason C. Eckhardt as well as the young and promising weird writer Farah Rose Smith, to whom Sam was something of a mentor. His unexpected death earlier this year, following a massive heart attack, renders it sadly possible that Smith's anthology *Machinations and Mesmerism* is the last book that this press will issue.

I fervently wish that this book was better than it is. Its seventeen contributors focus on key motifs in Hoffmann's work—the homunculus, the doppelgänger, the Gothic castle, and, of course, the mesmerism of the title (I have no idea what "machinations" could refer to in the context of Hoffmann's work or in that of the stories in the book)—but few of them do so with any compelling grasp of either narrative drive or prose idiom.

Some stories do stand out for commendation. Rhys Hughes's "No Half Measures" is another of his patented tales melding whimsicality and gruesomeness. Here we are confronted with the city of Chaud-Mellé, where a citizen with the piquant name of Scythrop Pavone believes that the city's economic activity is insufficient to support its size and population. He teams up with one Frabjal Troose to fold the city in half—literally. The tale is recounted with Hughes's customary abundance of fantastic imagination.

Effective in a quite different way is "Awake in the Hands of Solitude" by Kurt Newton and John Boden. Here, Cyril Von [*sic*] Foerster seeks to revive his dead wife Camille—or perhaps only her hands. This ultimately leads to the emergence of all manner of disembodied hands that wreak havoc among the protagonists. As an excursion into grisly body horror, the tale has considerable merit.

Jayaprakash Satyamurthy's "Alpha and Iota" vividly depicts a man, who identifies himself only as Alpha, learning to deal with his "smaller self," named Iota. How these two figures interact with Alpha's divorced wife, Gamma, and his estranged teenage daughter, Theta, is the focus of a haunting tale of domestic and supernatural horror.

L. C. von Hessen's "Heirloom" is a series of disparate narratives, some of a fairytale-like quality, that appear to have nothing to do with one another and generally deal with a woman who appears to have been turned into a doll. But the author cleverly unites the divergent strands at the end. Another fairytale-like story is Sandy Parsons's "Ladali," about a girl who receives a blank book from a friend; but the overall import of the story remains unclear. The same could be said for Sonya Taaffe's "Where the Sky Is Silver and the Earth Is Brass," a rambling and inconclusive colloquy between a Jewish woman and a demon.

K. H. Vaughan's "Unheimlich" is a gripping tale about the last days of Sigmund Freud and his family, as he is forced to flee Germany in 1938 and settle in London, where he died of cancer of the jaw on September 23, 1939. Although the tale does involve what appears to be an automaton that Freud had created to aid in psychoanalyzing himself, the most vivid facets of the story are its grim descriptions of Germany's bombing of England in the early stages of World War II. Readers unfamiliar with the fact that Freud's celebrated essay "The Uncanny" ("Das Unheimliche," 1919) was focused around Hoffmann's "The Sandman" would be justified in being puzzled as to the story's inclusion in this volume, since the editor fails to mention this connection between Freud and Hoffmann.

Michael Cisco's "Professor Homonculus [*sic*]," which deals with a professor of classics (the only member of his department) who may be a homunculus, has elements of interest and is blissfully free of the utter obscurity and opacity that plague many of the author's other works; but several elements of the story seem unresolved or not to have much to do with the central narrative. More effective is Jennifer Quail's "Deadhead," where a forensic odontologist who is carrying the skull of a dead man involved in a probate case has a disturbing colloquy with a flight attendant. Michelle F. Goddard's "The Polished Scope of Dragon Hide" is a strangely poignant post-apocalyptic tale in which some cataclysm has overwhelmed the earth, with the few remnants of humanity apparently living inside a mountain. A girl named Amelia builds a bicycle—a symbol of her desire to escape the settlement and venture out in the world, devastated as it may be. D. J. Moore's "Spinollio" is the mildly interesting story of a woman who falls in love with a singer who turns out to be an automaton, and who is then involved in a duel.

We reach close to the nadir in Ian Delacroix's "Dr. Ligett's Dream," a dream narrative in which the protagonist undergoes all manner of abuse, from being trapped in a cage to being on an operating table to having wings attached to him. The upshot of all these tribulations is never clarified, and the story is peppered with illiteracies. Much the same could be said for Aydan Hasanli's perfectly illiterate "A Woman from the Dark." It is painfully obvious that English is not the native language of these two writers (the former of whom is from Italy and the latter from Azerbaijan). Lest I be accused of ethnocentrism, I will be quick to note that any number of American- or English-born writers in our field create the vivid impression that English is not their native language.

Sam Gafford's work as author, critic, and publisher will remain in memory as long as there is interest in the weird. As a person, Sam was quiet and unassuming, perhaps feeling (unjustly) that he was not quite on the level of some of the more prominent figures in the field, even among his own circle; and he was understandably dismayed that the intrinsic merits of his work were not gaining him a wide following. But those who knew him will long recall his understated humor, his generosity in sharing his research, and his selfless devotion both to his wife, Carol, and to the literary causes he espoused. He will be remembered.

"I No Longer Live in This House": The Liminality of Undeath in the Works of R. Murray Gilchrist

Daniel Pietersen

The trope of the lost author is a well-worn one, but there are fewer authors more lost, in all senses of the word, than Robert Murray Gilchrist.

Born in Sheffield in 1867, Gilchrist was a prolific author of great stylistic breadth. By the time of his death in 1917, just before the end of the Great War, he had written over twenty novels, around one hundred short stories, and a handful of histories of the greater Peak District area. Gilchrist was also well known in society. He counted amongst his friends the likes of H. G. Wells and Hugh Walpole, who could trace his lineage back to *The Castle of Otranto*'s Horace Walpole.

Whilst long-form works like *Beggar's Manor* or *The Labyrinth* drew attention for their "morbid extravagance" (*Spectator*, 15 March 1902), Gilchrist's short stories were famed for their fantastical imagery and sinister gloom. Tales like "The Basilisk" or "The Crimson Weaver," published in the sixth issue of celebrated decadent literary periodical, the *Yellow Book,* alongside tales by Henry James and Kenneth Grahame, present eerily timeless depictions of horror. The fluid view that Gilchrist had of gender and sexuality, making male characters either feeble or feckless whilst female characters are decisive and driven, also gained him notice. Although unpalatable to some audiences in his day—the *Spectator* criticised Gilchrist's works for "containing far too much in the way of sensuous description" (28 February 1891)—the author Eden Phillpotts would later announce that "no record of the English story would be complete without a study of [Gilchrist's] contributions" (James Machin, *Weird Fiction in Britain 1880–1939* [Palgrave Macmillan, 2018]).

Yet, like many of his protagonists, a strange doom lingered around Gilchrist. He died suddenly at the relatively young age of fifty and, as Peter Sneddon notes in one of the few biographical fragments on Gilchrist, his "star dimmed almost to nothing after his death" ("The Life of Long-Lost Derbyshire Writer Robert Murray Gilchrist," *Derbyshire Life & Countryside,* 20 April 2015). None of his novels are now in print and only two collections of his short stories are easily available to modern readers. *A Night on the Moor* was published in 2006 as part of the Wordsworth Tales of Mystery and Suspense series before being dropped from the roster when the series was rebranded as Tales of Mystery and the Supernatural. *The Basilisk,* a collection published by Ash-Tree Press in 2003 which covers similar ground to the Wordsworth edition, can be found through specialist resellers at often inflated prices. Of his historical gazetteers there is barely a trace.

Hugh Lamb, who attempted a revival of the author's work in the 1970s, wrote that Gilchrist was "an unrecognised master of the macabre story" (*Tales from a Gas-Lit Graveyard* [Dover, 1979]). Yet Lamb's efforts came to nothing. Gilchrist's work remains largely unrecognized and, perhaps saddest of all, even Gilchrist's grave holds no hint that he ever wrote a word of prose in his life.

Why is this? A possible reason is that he simply didn't fit the popular idea of what he was expected to be or, at least, didn't fit it as well as others did. Gilchrist is lost today because he was, in many senses, lost in his own day.

While Gilchrist is often described as a decadent writer, he was anything but decadent himself. Unlike other decadents he shunned England's cities. Visits to London were made only occasionally, and he preferred the quietness of the countryside. At the time of "The Crimson Weaver"'s publication, a blood-red tale that talks of "wreaths of withering asphodels" and "steaming sanguine pools," he was living with his parents and sisters in Cartledge Hall, located in the Derbyshire village of Holmesfield. He is perhaps also the only so-called decadent who was a regular contributor to the *Abstainer's Advocate,* the journal of the British temperance movement. His one truly decadent facet is that he shared the rooms in his parents' home with George Garfitt, often euphemistically described in biographical fragments as a "male companion."

In fact, although Gilchrist's short work does feature decadent elements and themes—Dionysian intoxication and madness, an abhorrence of the self, and inverted moralities—it is perhaps more accurate to refer to it as a precursor of that blend of the Gothic, the horrifying, and the eerily hallucinatory that we now call weird fiction. It is telling that the year of Gilchrist's birth also saw the death of Baudelaire and that 1917, the year of Gilchrist's death, saw H. P. Lovecraft write "The Tomb," which is commonly considered to be his first piece of true weird fiction. I believe there is a strong argument that Gilchrist wasn't someone who fell into the cracks but who dwelt willingly within them, a liminal being who acted as a transition between two related modes of writing but who never fully existed in one or another. Gilchrist, in fact, was a liminal writer.

Liminality is a phrase coined by the ethnographer and folklorist Arnold van Gennep in his 1909 work *Rites of Passage* and is a way of describing the transition between two separate states of being. Liminality is often understood as the process by which two states or ways of being transition from one into the other, with a period of overlap. The word liminal comes from the Latin *limen,* a doorway of gateway, and it's easy to think of liminality as a direct transition from one room to the next, one state to the next.

However, van Gennep used it more subtly to describe the peculiar lack of state that lies at the heart of ritual initiation: during an initiation ceremony the petitioner is neither uninitiated nor initiated but lingers at some point in between. The petitioner possesses elements of both states but exists truly in neither and rather hovers in a liminal state. Bjorn Thomassen, a modern-day scholar of van Gennep, describes liminality as a way to explain how humanity "live[s] through the uncertainties of the in-between" (*Liminality and the Modern: Living through the In-Between* [Ashgate, 2014]). And, as much as we live through the in-between, we also die through it.

Undeath, neither true life nor true death but possessing elements of each, is almost textbook liminality. Revenants and ghosts are like the living, but they are not the living. They are like the dead, but they are not the dead. Gilchrist approaches this concept, as always, with great subtlety. He uses liminality to intimate undeath and, beyond that, uses undeath to intimate something even more taboo, especially for a male writer in his time period.

In "The Return," Gilchrist presents us with what is, at first glance, a relatively commonplace tale. An unnamed narrator leaves his beloved, the fair Rose Pascal, to make his fortune and returns years later only to find that she has passed away in his absence. So far, so Gothic. Yet Gilchrist uses a number of cues, buried within the narrative, to tell another story for those who wish to find it.

Our narrator returns to his home village of Halkton to find it falling into dereliction. People he once knew are now aged and distant or simply dead. He walks to Bretton Hall, Rose's home, and he finds a woman sitting alone, surrounded by an air of weary grief:

> A withered woman sat beside the peat fire. She held a pair of steel knitting needles which she moved without cessation. There was no thread on them, and when they clicked her lips twitched as if she had counted. Some time passed before I recognised her as Rose's foster-mother, Elizabeth Carless. The russet colour of her cheeks had faded and left a sickly grey; those sunken, dimmed eyes were utterly unlike the bright black orbs that had danced so mirthfully.

Here we meet the first undead, or perhaps unliving, entity in the tale. A withered figure, shrunken and sickly, who seems oblivious to the living world and exists in a state of feeble repetition. A remnant of what was once a human being yet not quite yet a ghost. She has become a liminal figure, neither of the world nor the grave. Recoiling in horror, our narrator moves to the Hall proper and, again, finds an undead thing— a rotten and decaying building that once bustled with the life of a family home. The furniture is described as having been "once so fondly kept, now mildewed and crumbling to dust," neither lost nor fully present. Finally, inevitably, he meets the third undead presence of the story Rose herself.

Unlike her foster-mother, Rose is lucid and emotional; she sobs piteously as she embraces her lover. Like her foster-mother, however, she has aged:

The red-and-yellow silk shawl still covered her shoulders; her hair still hung in those eldritch curls. But the beautiful face had grown wan and tired, and across the forehead lines were drawn like silver threads.

There is a nervousness in her manner. Her speech is laced with what is described as "a wild fear." She suddenly announces that "I no longer live in this house" before drawing the narrator away to an unhallowed place, described as "a veritable Golgotha" where the touch of "a cold hand" sends them both into a slumber. The narrator awakens alone to find that he has been sleeping on a stone marker which informs him that:

> Here, at four cross-paths, lieth, with a stake through the bosom, the body of Rose Pascal, who in her sixteenth year wilfully cast away the life God gave.

Rose is not only dead but has endured that most liminal of deaths: suicide.

This adds a shudder to "The Return" but is still not the true meaning of the story. For that need to look slightly further.

> Rose is buried at a cross-roads with a stake through her heart. This is ominous yet was not unusual for the time. The grave of real-life late 18th century suicide Kitty Jay, for example, is still to be found at a crossroads on Dartmoor in Devon. Folklore held that suicides would rest uneasily in death, no longer in the living world but also not allowed to pass into the afterlife. Being buried at a crossroads was, apparently, enough to confuse the spirit and stop them from rising from their graves to haunt friends or family. Even the use of a stake can be attributed to a wish to keep the corpse in its rightful place.

However, Gilchrist is well known for the use of mythic symbolism, especially the symbolism related to flowers and plants, to add greater depth to his short stories. As I discussed in a previous article ("Bestarred with Fainting Flowers," *Dead Reckonings* No. 21), Gilchrist often uses floral mythology to indicate subtle sub-plots in his work. The use of asphodels in "The Crimson Weaver," for example, links that story to the shadowy afterlife of Homeric myth where the plant covers the meadows of the dead and Persephone, Queen of the Dead, weaves its flowers into her hair. "The Return" is no different, and flower symbology again shows that he intended Rose to be more than a simple revenant.

At the very start of "The Return" the narrator describes a vignette where "beneath the oldest tree stood the girl I love, mischievously plucking yarrow, and, despite its evil omen, twining the snowy clusters in her black hair." The mention here of yarrow—also known as bloodwort, devil's nettle, and nosebleed, sanguinary and eerie—is not accidental. The plant's "evil omen" comes from its ability to both cause and staunch the flow of blood. Not only that, but excessive exposure to the plant can cause increased sensitivity to sunlight in human skin.

Photosensitivity, imbalanced blood chemistry, a burial at a crossroads, a corpse staked into its coffin. Is "The Return" really a vampire story?

Yes. Well, in a way.

Gilchrist made previous ventures into vampirism, but it is rarely the vampirism we might expect. "The Crimson Weaver," for example, uses the blood of her victims not to provide sustenance but to create her lustrous gowns. "The Return" is a story about an equally unexpected kind of vampire, but one that is no less draining.

It is a story about despair.

Gilchrist uses the notion of undeath in "The Return" to talk, briefly, about how it is to be lost in despair.

Despair manifests itself in many ways—as many ways as there are sufferers—but one of its overriding elements is a feeling of hopelessness and lifelessness, of not being fully in the world. Those who despair are not dead, but neither are they truly living; they exist in a liminal zone that has facets of both but is neither in their fullest states. To despair at its most abyssal ebb is to become unliving.

It is to become undead, and the undead of "The Return" embody this despair.

Elizabeth Carless, Rose's foster-mother, is the despair that comes from grief. She is alive but, with her soul hollowed out by the death of her daughter, appears to be far less than alive. The world is distant to her and she comforts herself with repetitious and pointless actions.

Bretton Hall is the despair that comes from loss, an emotion that is subtly different from grief. Grief is a kind of jealousy, the terror that comes from having things taken from you. Loss is more akin to envy, when others have what you do not.

Rose Pascal is the despair that comes from abandonment, which itself is a liminal lingering between grief and loss. Unlike her foster-mother, she is dead but appears alive, and her actions are not repetitious but driven and intentional.

Understanding these roles allows us to see that the story becomes a kind of Gothic doubling: the path that Rose's despair follows is then also followed by the despair of the narrator as he returns to encounter the grief, loss, and abandonment that awaits him in the village. "The Return" becomes the eternal recurrence of Nietzsche where "the eternal hourglass of existence is turned over again and again."

A suitably gloomy experience, but Gilchrist allows a ray of sunlight to pierce through.

By drawing our attention to the liminal elements in the story—undeath and despair—Gilchrist reminds us that these elements are transitory. They must be liminal because liminality is a transitional state. Rose's despair eventually ends; her last act is to clutch her beloved and her last words are "you are strong," a statement of the narrator's physicality but perhaps also a reminder of mental fortitude. She passes from her undead state to one of true death and is finally laid to rest. Similarly, the narrator, even as he enters into his own liminal state of despair, announces, "See how glad the world looks—see the omens of a happy future."

Gilchrist's intent, laid out in a mere six pages, is to show the inherent liminality of how we experience the world. We will journey, we will love, and we will grieve. And all this will pass. The good can become bad, but the bad will become good.

Gilchrist tells us that, even when it feels as if we are locked away with nothing but our own suffering, we will one day look up and suddenly see a way out. One day we will look at the walls that kept us trapped for so long, see them fall away, and say, "I no longer live in this house."

Fathoms of Tropes

Géza A. G. Reilly

The Sinking City. Frogwares. Bigben Interactive, 2019. $59.99, PlayStation 4, Nintendo Switch, Xbox One, Microsoft Windows.

It seems to be almost a golden age for Lovecraftian video games. In 2018 we had *Call of Cthulhu,* licensed by Chaosium, and in 2019 we have Frogwares' much-anticipated *The Sinking City*. Frogwares has made a name for itself mostly thanks to its Sherlock Holmes games, and anticipation for its Lovecraftian effort was based largely on that history. Does *The Sinking City* live up to its hype? Well, yes and no. We get precisely what we were offered with *The Sinking City,* but it turns out that what we were offered was not all that substantial.

In *The Sinking City,* players take on the role of Charles Reed, who has come to the city of Oakmont in order to investigate a recent outbreak of insanity. Hoping that his investigation will reveal the reason for his own nightmares, Reed is drawn into a web of overlapping mysteries and plots that ultimately put the world itself at risk. Reed is an interesting protagonist, with an engaging backstory of disaster aboard the *U.S.S. Cyclops,* and he is well acted. Unfortunately, he is not quite enough to save the game as a *Lovecraftian* game, nor does he excuse its technical deficiencies.

For *The Sinking City* is not solid on a technical level. The game is replete with bugs and glitches, and although none of them are game-breaking, they are nonetheless annoying to any dedicated player. If you cannot abide these flaws, or if you are not willing to forgive creators stemming from a small developer's studio consisting of less than one hundred people, then *The Sinking City* is not for you. If you *can* tolerate the sometimes comical flaws in light of the fairly detailed gameplay, serviceable plot, and thematic structures familiar to any Lovecraft (or, perhaps, Derleth) fan, then I'd recommend giving it a playthrough.

What I'm interested in exploring with this review is a larger question that I touched on in my *Call of Cthulhu* review. After spending a considerable amount of time completing every side-quest and the main quest of *The Sinking City*, I am forced to conclude that the game very much *looks and feels* Lovecraftian while not actually *being* very Lovecraftian at all. That is, like *Call of Cthulhu, The Sinking City* uses quite a bit of the window-dressing from Lovecraft, but not very much of the view. Some of that window-dressing is interesting—I was fascinated to find "Facts concerning the Late Arthur Jermyn and His Family" showing up, sort of, as a major impetus for several characters, for example—but I'm afraid that a passing fancy is all that it is.

What makes a Lovecraft story a *Lovecraft* story? This perennial question is at issue just as much as the often-asked "what makes weird fiction *weird* rather than *horror*?" When it comes to video games thus far released, including *The Sinking City,* I am afraid that I have to argue that the predominant genre is horror rather than weird. There is nothing really of Lovecraft in *The Sinking City* (or last year's *Call of Cthulhu*); the trappings are here, but trappings are all they are. The Esoteric Order of Dagon can be an interesting addition to a game's story, for example, on the level of making players who are in the know sit up and take notice of what has just been signposted . . . When that addition does not carry with it any of the underpinnings Lovecraft put into his idea of the EoD, however, the hollowness of the inclusion becomes noticeable.

Merely having something that is Cthulhu-like (by way of Derleth and Lumley) is not enough to make a story Lovecraftian any more than having a fanged vampire is sufficient to make a story Stokerian (to coin an adjective). *The Sinking City* has much that looks as if it could be ripped from Lovecraft's pages, but it's more the hollowed-out skin of a Lovecraft narrative—one that has been emptied of all meaning, philosophy, and structure. What we are left with is an enjoyable (the game *is* fun) but ultimately empty and forgettable experience. There are few frights in *The Sinking City* and, worse, there are no hints of newness here. The game does nothing, that is, with Lovecraftian video game tropes other than to arrange them in a pattern that we haven't quite seen before.

Can a video game be Lovecraftian? That is the question that I've been mulling over in the two months or so since I beat *The Sinking City*. I answered that question after beating *Call of Cthulhu* with a tentative yes, but now I must amend my thoughts to a fairly resounding "no." A game can look and sound Lovecraftian, and it can even be scary, but I am not, as of now, convinced that a video game can capture the frisson that a Lovecraft narrative—or even a narrative by one of his more talented disciples—manages to get across. I am loath to fall into the tired old "how can one represent the unrepresentable?" canard that's been leveled at Lovecraftian cinema since the middle of the last century, but I have to admit that if Lovecraftian video games want to work *completely,* they have to be dedicated toward giving us more than tentacled monsters and inbred tragedies. That is, video games are a necessarily visual medium, and nobody has yet figured out how to be *weird* with themes and structures without relying on only an appearance of similarity.

Is *The Sinking City* a memorable game? No, not really, though it has innovative ideas for detective investigation mechanics and multi-tiered plots influenced by player action. Is it a fun game? Certainly, if one can look past its technical flaws. Is it a Lovecraftian game? Yes, but largely in name only. Is it the game that finally gives us a truly weird experience beyond the limitations of *Anchorhead* or *Silent Hill 2*? No, not really, and thus I cannot recommend *The Sinking City* to the wider Lovecraftian fandom unless they are, like me, too starving for the real thing to care about the quality of the meal.

Were We Ever Innocent? Childhood Horrors of Knowledge and Sexuality in Gene Wolfe's Fiction

Marc Aramini

In April 2019, the Science Fiction and Fantasy community lost one of its most decorated and respected writers. The awards and recognitions Gene Wolfe received over the course of his career were a testament to both the enduring literary quality of his fiction and to the popularity he achieved despite a reputation for difficult texts that demanded significant (and perhaps unique) commitments from readers. For those fascinated by biographical detail, a more poetic or more effective introduction to Wolfe's early life cannot be found than Brian Phillip's "Gene Wolfe Turned Science Fiction into High Art," published mere weeks after Wolfe's death in the *Ringer* and readily available online. The lonely but evocative details that Phillips recounts of Wolfe's childhood might almost serve as a murky lens through which to view some of Wolfe's most chilling and effective short stories and novellas. Generally considered an eclectic fantasy author who occasionally dabbled in science fiction, Gene Wolfe was far more complex in reality. A glance at his total body of work should convince almost anyone that this is a fairly egregious oversimplification. In his fiction, Wolfe loved to play with the conventions of genre in unexpected but often still traditional ways, and his contribution to horror has been largely unappreciated.

One of the first important considerations of Wolfe as a writer involves determining, amidst some initial confusion, which genre conventions he employs in any given story. Of his approximately 225 short stories, 50 of them, and at least six of his over 30 novels, contain subject matter that one could consider, overtly or covertly, horrific in either subject or tone. While the scope of this article cannot hope to touch on all those stories in sufficient depth, there are a few features of

Wolfe's style that make even his non-horror writing echo with haunting and numinous resonance.

Upon first reading a Gene Wolfe story, many readers tend to experience disorientation. Some readers might even be tempted to conclude that the nebulous uncertainty of much of Wolfe's work will forever be inscrutable. However, almost from the start of his long and lauded career, Wolfe was clearly interested in some of the most immersive and meaningful aspects of traditional tale-telling. In his introduction to *Endangered Species* (1989), one of his best collections, he lays out some of his ideas about what a story should and should not be. Most importantly, he ties it to a tradition that is as old as human communication itself:

> [S]tories are far older than any classroom. They came to be at a time when the storyteller knew his (more correctly her, for the first were almost certainly women) audience thoroughly, and was not in the least averse to altering his narration to fit it. The hearer (every true reader hears the tale in his mind's ear) is more central than the monstrous beast slain on the other side of the mountains, or the castle upon the hill of glass . . .
>
> Tonight you and I, with billions of others, are sitting around the fire we call "the sun," telling stories; and from time to time it has been my turn to entertain. I have occasionally remembered that though you are not a child, there is a child alive in you still, for those in whom the child is dead will not hear stories.

Even with this invocation of the oldest storytelling traditions and Wolfe's obvious affection for the idea of the inner child, there is something devious in the construction of his typical stories, and nowhere is this more apparent than in those often horrifying tales that feature as their protagonists the very young. There seem to be two consistent forces at work on many of his young main characters: one the allure of stories and traditions, the other the terrible knowledge of sex, almost always tied to cruelty, violence, or violation.

One of the most important hallmarks of Wolfe's style involves his ability to imply on an almost subconscious level. Sometimes an unseen horror, unfettered and unbound by the senses, is far more effective than the visceral descriptions of gore or even a clear picture of the monster lurking around the corner. It is the unknown and the unknowable that can quicken both hope and terror in a human audience, and often the most sublime portrayals of mystery and horror loom tantalizingly just beyond our collective grasp. Wolfe's narratives almost always have their fingers on the pulse of potential. Self-knowledge and full understanding represent some of the biggest obstacles for Wolfe's mature heroes, but there is a very different threat at work in the burgeoning knowledge of the young, encountering a world they apprehend dimly and only in part, but from which they remain almost universally isolated as fully functioning and participating members.

Wolfe's fiction explores potentials with great regularity. Many of his tragic characters, especially those featured in what might be considered horror stories, are young children. The most overt of his fantastic stories, "Queen of the Night" (1994), features a main character stolen from his home by carrion-eating ghouls. The story even features his sexual grooming by that fey force. Wolfe's first serious award contender, "The Island of Doctor Death and Other Stories" (1970), was also concerned with maturation and revealed, in much more subtle fashion, the horror of neglected and forgotten childhood, in which the second-person protagonist of the story, Tackman Babcock, is primarily left to his imagination and his books to help understand and contextualize the events happening around him. These events include his mother's drug abuse and the presence of her possibly abusive (and certainly insulting) boyfriend in his life.

However, none of Wolfe's stories is more horrific than the prosaically and almost banally titled "Houston, 1943" (1988). The main character, a young boy named Roddie, whose life parallels Gene Rodman Wolfe's life to an enormous degree, seems to have been trapped in a dreamlike state, his awareness or spirit separated from his body even as forces conspire to kidnap and use that body to their own end. While the text follows a kind of dream logic, "Houston, 1943" must be one of the most terrifying things Wolfe has ever written. It is even more jarring given its simple title, one that invokes an ordinary day in Texas when Gene Rodman "Roddie" Wolfe would have been twelve years old. Instead, the dread and horror of dreams, visions, and uncertainty are captured in a way that gives readers insight into both the fears of Wolfe's childhood and the transmutation fantasy tropes undergo in his subconscious. From the works of Poe to the characters in *Treasure Island* and *Peter Pan,* Wolfe's childhood reading is brought to life in visceral and unexpected ways. In his introduction to *Innocents Aboard* (2005), Wolfe writes:

> "Houston, 1943" is sort of autobiographical. I grew up in Houston, with a very nice mama and a very nice daddy and a fat spaniel named Boots. In 1943, I was twelve; and that's my family, my bedroom, and so forth. There were bugs and tarantulas, alligators, poisonous snakes, Nazi submarines, and housemaids who practiced voodoo. All of that is real.

In the story, we see a sinister figure compared to Santa Claus (though probably thinner than the sexually exploitative abductor at the conclusion of Wolfe's disturbing "And When They Appear" [1993]), the hand of glory that returns in Wolfe's novel *The Land Across* (2013), the haunting pirate of "The Gunner's Mate" (2005), the voodoo of *Home Fires* (2011), the overactive imagination of a lonely boy in "The Island of Doctor Death and Other Stories," and even the fragmentation into multiple parts and personalities that some of Wolfe's most famous protagonists undergo (such as Severian from *The Book of the New Sun* [1980–83], Silk in *The Book of the Short Sun* [1999–2001], and possibly even Able in *The Wizard Knight* [2004]). All these things lived in Wolfe's imagination as a child, in the raw images of nightmares haunted by other stories.

There is a discernible plot to the text, in which Roddie, primarily a being of spirit throughout the tale, attempts to rejoin his body, which has been captured by the antagonists. This surreal separation of spirit and matter is contextualized by Voodoo Petro, or black magic. Motivated by greed, the antagonists Doc and Sheba have summoned other spirits in order to gain a treasure, but those forces are intent on a quite different goal (either a peaceful burial or, more probably, permanent possession of a young body in order to live again). Wolfe's use of Haitian voodoo highlights his naturally syncretic sensibilities. The traditional Catholic symbols in voodoo invoke very different powers *behind* them. Thus, someone ignorant of those transmutations might interrupt a ceremony and see only a lithograph of a Catholic saint, while something entirely different is being invoked. The surface *looks* like one thing and actually signifies another, and, in this story's possible allegory of maturity and change, much of the narrative drama involves the risk of Roddie losing who he really is, with the threat of a different spirit animating his body. He will still look like Roddie, just as the images of voodoo are identical to Catholicism, but the soul attached to that physical representation will have been completely altered.

Even though Houston in 1943 must have seemed like a normal community, Wolfe's story also allows the subtle cultural uneasiness of his childhood to contribute to the atmosphere. Segregated beaches, the threat of a Nazi attack, and even sinister rituals all add to the inexorable and lurking menace of the story. Perhaps one of the historical events in the background is also the Surprise Hurricane of 1943, so called because of the censorship of the news media during World War II, which prevented warning and preparation for the extreme storm and proved disastrous. People simply had no idea they were in danger. Without the ability to see threats clearly, one does not know how to respond. Sheba and Doc seem motivated by greed, but in their use of voodoo they bring spirits with far more malevolent motives. Though the character Jim (a manifestation from the pages of *Treasure Island*) claims they want to be laid to rest, they are very interested in Roddie's body.

The most horrifying aspect of the story is that once the subconscious sleeping mind has been awoken, it seems unable to return to the normal world of day, forever trapped in an unending night where anything and everything is possible, no matter how unsettling. While the events are dreamlike, on a deeper level the passage of time and the accrual of life experiences (or reading experiences) have transformed the Houston of 1943 into a threatening and eldritch place for Roddie.

One of the story's mysteries involves the identity of a boy sacrificed in a rite. While Roddie is clearly a stand-in for Wolfe, perhaps the sacrificed boy also represents something of the innocence lost in growing up and becoming haunted by terrifying stories and supernatural dread. The harrowed spirit of the sacrificed boy might become the mature storyteller Wolfe, while the more innocent Roddie is trapped out in a dark night which never ends. The sleeper looks at the world with the same eyes, but much as in the syncretism of Catholicism and voodoo, a different, darker spirit animates his body. The creatures and characters in the supernatural and adventure stories Wolfe read have come alive and, by the harrowing conclusion, *the worlds of imagination have become the real world*. In this regard, the story is thematically closest to "The Island of Doctor Death and Other Stories," but there is none of the developing empathy between fictional character and child that redeems Tackman Babcock's experiences as he interacts with characters from his books who help him contextualize his real-world experiences.

An even more revolting fate awaits Sherby, the young protagonist of Wolfe's science fictional "And When They Appear" (1993). His parents have attempted a suicide ultimately thwarted only for him by the automated house, which has become his guardian and only refuge from an increasingly violent and riotous world; the poor and discontented have risen up to destroy those whom they consider to be better off. Even though Wolfe has effectively eradicated entire planetary populations in at least one of his books, this story has his most disturbing and controversial conclusion: young Sherby's fate, sexual abuse at the hands of a corpulent man dressed as Santa Claus, is exceptionally cruel. Wolfe's concluding comments on the story in *The Best of Gene Wolfe* (2009) throw some doubt on its actual genre:

> We associate ghost stories with Halloween now ... but ghosts at Christmas are far older. The three seen by Ebenezer Scrooge are not the beginning but almost the end of a lengthy tradition. If you were to return as a ghost, wouldn't you rather revisit your family at Christmas?
>
> So I hope you noticed the ghosts, and that you noticed (as only a few readers do) that there is an anti-Santa, too. Poor Sherby rejects Santa Claus and gets someone much worse.

While the story seems to be dystopian near-future SF, in the decay of an affluent and sheltered environment with automated and opulent mansions (Sherby has a five-car garage, after all), "And When They Appear" mixes mythical and fantastic elements. The house, sometimes referred to as House, has decided to provide Christmas entertainment for the boy by manifesting various Christmas traditions and lore. There is even some reason to doubt that some of the spirits of Christmas, including Knecht Rupprecht, Christmas Rose, and Loki, are pure creations of House. Sherby asks to invite Santa Claus and his elves as well, and Wolfe of course plays on this by having the companions of Saint Nicholas from multiple traditions arrive, in all their ambiguity, showing the tension inherent in Christmas itself, when a pagan date married to the winter solstice was appropriated to Christian ends in a kind of eternal and cosmic fertility ritual. The date heralds a birth destined for sacrifice to ensure renewal and redemption, but only through death, and, in the case of our ancestral spirits given a voice by Loki, it is a re-enactment of necessary placation. It appears that Sherby's innocence is the sacrifice required this year, and the conclusion of the story makes all too clear exactly why humanity needs a metaphysical redemption and renewal in its muted exploration of a horrific abuse. Not only must Sherby join in the beating and probable murder of his "favorite" present, a mule, he must then face the concupiscent Corporal Charlie (one wonders if the title Corporal summons a corporeal, anti-spiritual reality and desire as well as a rank).

Once again in this story, there is a tension between the "fantasy" characters and the intrusion of real danger, but even the fiercest of House's illusions cannot save Sherby from his fate. Wolfe has explicitly worked against this kind of conclusion in "The Adopted Father" (1980), where the protagonist's fantasy effectively protects a child from the harsh truth of his mother's suicide and the violent overtures of a small gang, who do not know how to respond to an eccentrically creative threat. Sometimes fantasy and figurative truths have power in Wolfe. In any case, the Christmas stories projected and retold by House fail to save Sherby from the sexual exploitation of an older man, in whose clutches he is left at the end of the story (though at least there is some small hope that he might not be trapped forever). Wolfe's statements about the story seem to ascribe some responsibility to Sherby for choosing the anti-Santa over believing in the benevolent spirit of Christmas; Sherby's fate highlights exactly why mankind needs a savior.

There are many other young protagonists with a strange relationship with sex in Wolfe's stories, from the isolated and abandoned main character of "Josh" (2011), who is provoked to murder at a backwards glance from a girl in whom he is interested after she shows up with her boyfriend at his empty house, to the oddly puritanical main character of "It's Very Clean" (1972), in which a visit to an automated brothel for a young boy turns into a fleshly sexual experience that brings out sympathy in the girl working there toward him but only horror, revulsion, and meanness in the boy. Another odd Wolfe story, "Pocketsful of Diamonds" (2000), features the phantasmagoric experiences of a young brother and sister in foster care, who seem to encounter and overcome aggressive shadow versions of themselves. There is an unsettling moment in which the symbols of the text appear to suggest a kind of sexual knowledge that the siblings come to, symbolically illustrated through the sensual consumption of a candy apple, perhaps resonant with the knowledge of good and evil. (David Apple and Candi Cotin are the names of the shadowy and threatening new arrivals who try to take the sleeping quarters of the main characters Danny and Debbie.) In what could very well be a companion piece, the story "Mute" (2002) also has a horrific texture and quality.

"Mute" features rather straightforward action: a young girl and her brother are isolated and alone, with the rest of humanity oddly absent; they are unable to ascertain exactly what has happened. Just like "Pocketsful of Diamonds," "Mute" seems to be highly symbolic, experimenting with one of the ultimate isolation stories, echoing Adam and Eve alone in Eden, choosing to ignore the safety measures that their Father has put in place for them. When they come to their empty residence, the television has been muted; all they can do is watch fragmented scenes of disaster without hearing the actual words. Jill's father might very well have muted the television to protect them from the truth of what has happened to the world and the knowledge of an evil reality, but the siblings' metaphysical situation is probably not quite so simple. The appearance of this story in the anthology *Wastelands: Stories of the Apocalypse* (2008) lends some credence to it as a post-apocalyptic survival story, after a disease wipes out most of the population, but there are still a few eerie or supernatural elements that should be considered.

Wolfe says, "'Mute' was written to show that horror need not wallow in blood and wrap itself in the bowels of its victims, that loneliness, isolation, and vulnerability can be more than sufficient" (Gregson). Thus we see that this is definitely a horror story, but we should also account for the seemingly fragmentary nature of Jill and Jimmy's memories. (They fail to recognize that Poplar Hill is their house, and Jill's memories of her mother and of the place they came from are very vague.) There might be enough support in the story to assume that their father, infected with a potential plague that has obliterated the human population of the earth, has gone to the basement to die and perished before Jill and her brother ever arrived home, though they occasionally catch a glimpse of his spirit. He might mute the television to prevent them from hearing of the illness and to protect them. Are the siblings in the real world or are they experiencing something more like an afterlife, an echo of reality or an ontological imitation replaying the manner in which they lived and possibly died?

The actions of their father, who has seemingly commissioned the bus driver to deliver them to a house that they do not recognize, might be protective. If a plague has decimated the earth, he is trying to provide for them even if he dies, and to maintain their innocence by preventing the news from reaching them. However, they fail to recognize that they cannot escape, and wind up returning to their starting point even as they flee the house. Wolfe even introduces a kind of incestuous theme at the end, where the brother and sister might hope to repopulate the world like Adam and Eve, but the likely trajectory of the story is that they will probably accomplish nothing but a few nights of warmth (or, conversely and metaphorically, infinitely many nights of very great warmth).

According to the website for the *Wastelands* anthology in which the story was reprinted:

Wolfe's story for *Wastelands*, "Mute"—which first appeared in the program book for the 2002 World Horror Convention, where Wolfe was guest of honor—was inspired by watching a muted television, Wolfe said. "I generally mute commercials, and often mute shows," he said. "At times, it can be interesting to try to figure out just what is going on, and it spares me from the canned laughter of the sitcoms."

"Mute" is about two children who return home, find an empty house—and their father dead—and are forced to grow up in a hurry, Wolfe said. "Jill is a girl who will probably begin menstruation within a year, an intelligent and resourceful child still very much in the shadow of her older brother," he said.

It is a considerable challenge to write an honest story in which the principal characters are as young as Jill and her brother, Wolfe said. "Children are not angels, devils, or short adults. . . . There is a breathtaking simplicity and purity. My research consisted largely of observing children, talking to them whenever possible, and occasionally questioning teenagers about their childhoods."

In writing "Mute," Wolfe drew upon his own childhood a great deal, he said. "People today almost never leave small children alone in the house. . . . It wasn't like that when I was child. My father was away from home almost every week from Monday morning until Friday night—he was a salesman covering an enormous territory—Texas, Oklahoma, and Louisiana—by car. We had no relatives in Texas. My mother often left me alone in the house for half a day or more while she shopped, went to the dentist, or whatever. On weekends, my parents would play bridge at the house of some other bridge-playing couple; I was often in bed and asleep by the time they returned." (Adams)

Wolfe goes on to note that post-apocalyptic fiction is interesting because of the individual power it explores:

> [P]ower is the chief appeal of post-apocalyptic fiction. "Most of us have very little control over our lives and our environments. . . . We must work to eat, and take whatever jobs we can get. Our votes do not matter because the men and women who are supposed to represent us could scarcely care less about our situations or opinions. We must live by the mores

of our society—mores we cannot reshape; and we long at times for a simpler, rougher age." (Adams)

This lets us see the action of the story as one exploring a sudden and unexpected freedom from all social expectation and roles, and the union Jill forms with her brother, as the younger and weaker gravitates to the stronger for protection, seems to become the relationship of a mate who seeks to cling to security, promising domestic duties such as cleaning and cooking in return for safety. Her father attempted to provide this security by hiding the problem and sequestering himself away to die. Now she needs a more physical and lively way to overcome her vulnerability, and her fears of being separated from Jimmy are clearest when he leaves her to try and scale a wall on his own.

As in much of Wolfe's fiction, it is possible to speculate on what has actually happened. In an apocalyptic realist reading, Jimmy and Jelly, as she is called, are almost the last two survivors on earth. Their father has acted to preserve them by somehow attaining a large estate that "fits" him, and his attempts to protect them from the truth leave them alone, where, free from social expectations and mores, they can do whatever they want to try to overcome their powerlessness. Conversely, this story might be merely an echo of the final days Jimmy and Jelly lived, in which their father tried to protect them from the truth, though they actually caught the sickness anyway, either from the coughing bus driver taking them home or from their father's corpse. They may have actually died when they tried to escape (possibly becoming the dead man and woman in the road featured on one of the channels). This would make the story very close to Wolfe's novel *Peace* (1975) in theme and execution and would also explain the gaps in Jill's memories, the strange description of the bus as something that might not be a bus, "although it was shaped like a bus and of a bus-like color."

Another reading might be that they have simply died, not necessarily of any plague, but of just about anything, even perhaps a bus accident, and are being punished for incestuous explorations or curiosities. The two alternatives above, with an actual plague their father was trying to protect them from, constitute a more holistic reading. The incest in that case is simply a natural outgrowth of fear and isolation—to whom can Jill turn for protection, and how can she actually ensure that continued shield? In some ways, this story might be a primal exploration of that need to feel safe by clinging to another adult to create a sane environment in a world quite beyond our control.

It is conceivable that there is nothing supernatural about the siblings' return to the house. Clearly the Christian imagery at work is one that directly invokes the story of Adam and Eve in the Garden of Eden, and Jill's increasing knowledge and maturity come to fruition in a world where it is possible to jump social fences and boundaries, for humanity itself has disappeared. Jimmy's uses a dead tree to clear the wall and approach his father's house from a different side, unknowingly. This might be a symbolic representation of the incestuous knowledge the two will soon learn to overcome the obstacle facing them. In plainer terms, jumping the fence of the property directly parallels their willingness to leap over old taboos in forging a new home—though it is ultimately identical to the old one in its hierarchical cruelty and unfairness.

Pirate Freedom (2007), *The Fifth Head of Cerberus* (1972), and even *The Book of the New Sun* (1980–83) also feature young characters thrust into cruel and possibly exploitative positions, and it is worth emphasizing that, while many read his work as a complex postmodern challenge to ultimate truth and objective experience, the construction of much of his fiction might almost be said to mirror that of the most orthodox theodicy. Much as Milton implied in *Paradise Lost* that he hoped to justify the ways of God to man, so that readers could understand, emotionally if not logically, that all bad things serve a greater purpose in the long run, Wolfe's most mature works serve exactly the same function. The terror and death in *Urth of the New Sun* (1987) are robbed of their permanent power by the promise that all things will eventually serve a greater good; humans are limited in their point of view, but something survives the death of the body, just as renewal comes to a dying planet, though not without significant change. In this manner, the free will of those who choose evil or selfishness still eventually comes to serve a greater good.

How ironic, then, that in almost every situation featuring a young protagonist in Wolfe's fiction, it is very hard to ascertain exactly where they might act decisively for good. They are trapped, abused, isolated, and often forced to struggle with situations that children should never have to encounter. It is almost as if this tension between free will and the helplessness of childhood exists in Wolfe's work subconsciously: even as his adult characters make decisions and struggle with their own perceptions, his children are constantly denied the space and freedom to save themselves from disaster. Powerless, self-motivated, but almost never truly innocent and childlike as his characters are, the loneliness and isolation of childhood prods Wolfe over and over into creating horrific and disturbing scenarios in which stories and knowledge are balanced against an almost perverse sexuality. Children cannot be defended from the knowledge of good and evil, even if they are powerless to do anything with that knowledge.

Hopefully Wolfe's contribution to the field of horror will be evaluated more widely in the near future. Despite his assertion that for stories to be heard and understood we must still have a child who lives inside us, his actual portrayal of children might leave us questioning the very idea that any kind of innocence is possible in this world.

Works Cited

Adams, John Joseph. "Wastelands." *Johnjosephadams.com*. 2015. 16 November 2015. www.johnjosephadams.com/wastelands/authors/ gene-wolfe/

Gregson, Anna. "Wastelands." Orbit Books. 13 June 2013. 16 November 2015. www.orbitbooks.net/2013/06/13/wastelands-featuring-stephen-king-george-r-r-martin-neil-gaiman-joe-hill-cory-doctorow-and-many-others/

Phillips, Brian. "Gene Wolfe Turned Science Fiction into High Art." *The Ringer*. 25 April 2019. www.theringer.com/2019/4/25/18515675/gene-wolfe-science-fiction-author

Wolfe, Gene. *The Best of Gene Wolfe*. New York: Tor Books, 2009.

———. *Endangered Species*. New York: Orb Books, 2004.

———. *Innocents Aboard: New Fantasy Stories*. New York: Tor Books, 2004.

"We Make Ourselves out of Stories, Y'Know?"

Karen Joan Kohoutek

ERIC J. GUIGNARD. *Doorways to the Deadeye*. n.p.: JournalStone, 2019. 312 pp. $18.95 tpb. ISBN 978-1-947654-97-6.

Sometimes it's hard to overcome the first impression you have of a work and judge it fairly on its own terms. For genre works in particular, it's not uncommon for them to face the obstacle of readers who won't give horror or fantasy a chance at all. But even fans of these genres all have individual prejudices and expectations within subgenres. In general, it's easier to be won over by something you didn't expect to like, once convinced to give it a chance, than it is to expect something you knew you wanted and then get something different.

Which is a long-winded way of saying that I want to be fair to this novel, since I think there are people out there who would like it, but it would probably help for them to know what they're getting into. In my case, the mere overall subject matter of Eric J. Guignard's novel *Doorways to the Deadeye,* a supernatural tale about hobos and the Hobo Code in the Great Depression, led me to expect another kind of book, which unfortunately made it hard for me to enjoy it for what it is.

Obviously, of course, it's true that "supernatural" doesn't mean spooky or eerie or even necessarily scary, but this is something very off to one side: in the same genre, say, as Richard Matheson's *What Dreams May Come* or the television series *Dead Like Me,* fictions that explore ideas about an afterlife and how it works, which is a different feel from most works that involve the supernatural in some form.

A cover blurb about Guignard's status as a Bram Stoker Award winner also led me to expect something spookier or more clearly in the horror genre. There are scenes in the book in which characters are menaced, and there are some unsettling images of beings and objects disintegrating into a formless void, but I found it more philosophical than horrific.

The novel follows hobo Luke Thacker, who has a unique ability to understand the underlying realities of existence. He has a knack for spotting and interpreting secret messages in the symbols of the real-life Hobo Code, a system used to pass messages among the transient men and women who travel the nation's railroads. His ability is shown to be mystical in nature when he spots some unusual glyphs—one the sideways figure eight of the infinity sign, and one an open door—that lead him into the "Deadeye," a place he comes to know as Athanasia. Here, the spirits of the dead continue an existence based on the memories of them that survive in the living world, as insubstantial beings, unseen by most living people, a "wispy trace of our old selves," as Harriet Tubman tells him.

Yes, it's that Harriet Tubman. The Athanasian society is dominated by those who are still well known in normal, everyday life, and myths and stories, existing as a form of fictionalized memory, have the power to shape reality on both planes of existence. As such, numerous historical figures appear in the novels, some as friendly acquaintances and some as avatars of evil.

Faced with the loss of loved ones, Luke tries to use his powers to keep them alive in Athanasia by turning them into stories. His inability to make other hobos care about the memory of his friend, who had experiences similar to their own, offers an insightful twist on the common idea that people only care about others who are like themselves. An audience may not want stories of the common people, who don't capture their imagination, preferring the outrageous adventures of glamorous, larger-than-life personalities.

Guignard makes some valuable points about the priority given to celebrities and historical "great men" for their exaggerated and sometimes completely fictional deeds, which detracts from the memory of regular people and their common struggles. Somewhat ironically, however, his introduction of more and more historical figures draws attention away from the characters in the foreground of the plot. By the time the fifth or sixth one showed up, I was finding their presence a distraction from what I had originally wanted, however unfair that probably is: something about the life of hobos, with a supernatural edge.

I'll add that there's a repetitive rhythm to many of the sentences, so on any page, many of the paragraphs begin with the construction of Luke's name, plus a verb as the start of new paragraphs within a few pages: "Luke nodded . . . Luke ran in front . . . Luke thought . . . Luke continued . . . Luke entered . . . Luke looked . . . Luke obliged." It's so prevalent that it seems purposeful, maybe as a form of plain-talking straightforwardness, but after a while I found this distracting too.

Overall, there are interesting ideas to be had here, and when I described it to a friend as being in the same subgenre as *What Dreams May Come,* she was immediately more interested in it than I had been, so that may be a useful comparison for its potential readers. In the meantime, I'm going to go look for a book about hobos with a spookier ambiance.

Recollections on NecronomiCon 2019

Edward Guimont

NecronomiCon has always been special to me, but the 2019 convention will now have a permanent position as a milestone not only in my professional development, but my life. It was in some ways the second act in a long weekend. On August 22, the Thursday before I went to Providence, I defended my doctoral dissertation. (One member of my defense committee I met at a separate conference also hosted at the Omni Hotel in 2018, in between NecronomiCons, which felt propitious.) On Friday, the 23rd, I sat on the "Eldritch Excavations" panel with Jeff Shanks and Rusty Burke and got the chance to talk not only about my dissertation topic—the medieval southern African city of Great Zimbabwe, and the speculative theories Europeans came up with to 'explain' its origins—but also a personal interest: ancient aliens. This was not only my first time participating in a non-Armitage event at NecronomiCon, but also my formal unveiling to the world as Dr. Guimont, something that I am very glad could happen at NecronomiCon. What's more, it was an excellent discussion, and one that I was happy to see clearly resonated with the attendees. The door man at Trinity Brewhouse even mentioned it when I entered for the Innsmouth Sea Shanties. When brewery staff recognize you, you know you've made it!

Saturday saw me chairing the Armitage "Literary & Philosophical Studies" panel—the first time I've chaired an academic panel, so another first of mine associated with NecronomiCon! Elena Tchougounova-Paulson, Jim Lethbridge, Christian Roy, and Sean Moreland each presented amazing research, and I was proud to help facilitate them in discussing it, especially as I have enjoyed many of their presentations.

Finally, Sunday saw my own Armitage presentation on Lovecraft in Connecticut. I want to thank Ian Fetters for stepping in as chair, along with Michael Torregrossa and Ben

Davis for their brilliant scholarship—I feel all three of us had very complementary research. I am also thankful to the questions from Donovan K. Loucks, and the information we've since exchanged over email. But I am especially grateful that Mike Bielawa and I met through attending each other's panels. I feel very strongly that we will have many years of fruitfully documenting and promoting the weird history of Connecticut together, and could not be more excited to work with him on that project.

That evening, I met with a graduate student from what I must now call my alma mater, and then drove back to prepare for teaching my first class of the semester on Monday, with NecronomiCon 2019 as the transition point from my defense to my teaching. I already cannot wait to see how 2021 will top it!

One postscript: NecronomiCon this year ran the same span as Disney's D23 Expo. What a tribute to Niels Hobbs, that Bob Iger is now forced to steal his convention thunder!

You Know Who the Monster Is

Michael D. Miller

S. L. EDWARDS. *Whiskey and Other Unusual Ghosts*. n.p.: Gehenna & Hinnom Books, 2019. 163 pp. $16.99 tpb. ISBN 978-1-950642-09-0.

"Contains 0% Sam L. Edwards." Unless you converse within certain circles in the weird community this slogan may mean very little, but to those few, the disclaimer is an in-joke among the publisher and contributors of *The Audient Void: A Journal of Weird Fiction and Dark Fantasy*. According to legend, Edwards pummeled the editor, Obadiah Baird, with submissions that had been rejected steadily over the first seven issues of the magazine. This eventually played out in the publication's first single-author edition issue featuring the work of David Barker and "0% Sam L. Edwards," with the aftermath resounding on social media among core contributors, from art director Dan Sauer to K. A. Opperman, Ashley Dioses, Adam Bolivar, and others. I am happy to report that this mock disclaimer no longer applies as Edwards will be appearing in issue #8 of the journal, and deservedly so as *Whiskey and Other Unusual Ghosts* shows the singular voice and talent of a formidable writer.

For a first collection of stories, Edwards has already attracted a fair number of prominent supporters from Gwendolyn Kiste, who provides the introduction, to S. P. Miskowski, Jon Padgett, Nadia Bulkin, and other luminaries. The book itself is very personalized, with author's notes after each story (which may perhaps spoil the mystery for some readers), black-and-white woodcut-style illustrations by Yves Tourigny for every story (and one of the author), and an afterward where Mr. Edwards does remind us that haunting is not an action unique to ghosts alone but also to "things that leave long lasting scars on the characters." In another added touch, asterisk marks breaking up time changes within the narrative are replaced with various whiskey bottles (each one completely unique throughout the collection). Monsters feature prominently in all the stories, though these are not the traditional real or imagined monsters used in horror literature but instead represent the internal pain and suffering of human beings, creating a bestiary of monstrosity with names such as abuse, addiction, depression, happiness, loneliness, and even love.

As for the writing and narrative, the collection shows a wide variation of storytelling, all held together by the deep cuts from wounded lives the various characters internally struggle with. Opening the collection is "Maggie Was a Monster," which boldly takes the risk of writing in the second-person, all the more risky for the opening story, as this point of view often throws off many readers. Edwards handles it with precision, for what better way to voice the monster of addiction and the internal struggle upon the character afflicted by the disease. Many addicts express their awareness of their condition as a conversation with themselves, internally and externally, the person they want to be and the addict they succumb to, two conflicted aspects of one being. Addiction is one monster statistics will confirm many of us know all too well.

Another monster familiar to most of us is love. "I've Been Here a Very Long Time" explores the haunting of, if not love, then the need to be happy (which some, including a few of the characters, confuse as love), becoming a theme resonating through many stories. In section I, we are initially enveloped in the childhood point of view of Carl and his encounters with a "monster" that is essentially the void created between himself and his parents' abusive relationship. The opening paragraph of this story demonstrates a refined skill at putting us into a character immediately, and is held successfully over the remaining sections (II–IV) as we follow Carl into adulthood, the monster still with him. One skill Edwards has honed in this collection is varying long and short sentences to immerse us in the ominous crawl of time: "At seven a.m. Carl sat up and looked at his closet door, closed completely. He stared at it until nine a.m." and "He walked to the front door and pulled the nob. Locked. Sighing, Carl looked at the clock. Five a.m."

"When the Trees Sing" takes us back to a second-person narration, this time through a military veteran suffering from

PTSD; however, varying on what is becoming an unfortunate trope, the protagonist suffers PTSD from trauma endured in his civilian life—deaths of his daughters and wife. Allusions to Dante's *Inferno* haunt the narrator's journey, reminding us the horror is the true story of the narrator's past. "And the Woman Loved Her Cats" gives us a terrifying spin on the "cat lady" trope. A character named Joe is assigned to the staff of the Higgins estate, currently populated by the Madame's cat hoard, led by a beast of a feline named Behemoth. The cats in this tale have acquired a taste for flesh, and Joe soon finds himself the only staff member willing to remain under the territorial torment of the cats that eventually take the life of the Madame. The story has obvious nods to H. P. Lovecraft's adoration of felines ("The Cats of Ulthar" and perhaps "The Rats in the Walls"). Behemoth is, according to Edwards, "the talking cat from Mikhail Bulgakov's *Master and Margherita* . . . much more malevolent in this incarnation." (Yet one can't help but sense *Sunset Boulevard* lurking on the fringes. After all, the protagonist's name is Joe and has hired himself to the "Madame" in an old mansion to help pay off his debts.)

The opening paragraph as central to any great story has been a hallmark of weird literature since Stephen King proclaimed Shirley Jackson's *The Haunting of Hill House* as having the best opening paragraph ever written. Edwards follows this tradition throughout *Whiskey and Other Unusual Ghosts*. Consider this gripping example from "Movie Magic":

> The Haunted Palace Cinema was plagued with premature ghosts. Urban legends clung to the building like remoras, sucking out business only to bring in cult followings. The theater was in an old district of town, a part of the world where businesses died and buildings stayed empty forever. Whether they remained empty out of respect, or out of viral desolation, was impossible to tell. The Haunted Palace attracted devoted fans whom flocked from all over the country to see obscure and wonderful movies of the horror variety. The fans fed it and the theater stood open, wearing its decay as ritual costume.

The story itself is an interesting mash-up of interactive theater and the "lost film" trope with a touch of cosmic vengeance, as the protagonist is consumed by "lovers of horror" and those who live horror. "The Case of Yuri Zaystev" begins with another best opening paragraph contender:

> Days were measured in piling snow, lives in black-rotting cells and time in final breath. The white-washed landscape was the endless world. To walk there, in that terrible and featureless place, was to take one more step toward heaven or hell. To stay there was to cosign fate to the primal elements that were both God and Devil. The tundra existed before man walked, before reptiles crawled the ocean floor, and would be there when the sun blotted out and the earth became silent.

This is one of the stand-out stories in the collection, concerning a "coffin-truck" driver in Stalin's Siberia. It is a wholly fascinating idea of "landscape horror," cold and isolating as Jack London, insulated in the howling wind of cosmic isolation.

"Golden Girl," with its subtle nods to *The King in Yellow* and Thomas Ligotti, delivers the goods on the terrors of adolescent love. In this sense, "falling in love is weird." "Primal adolescence was clawing at the back of his mind, and he hated every moment of it. Silently, mentally, he began hoping that God or Nature would intervene before he made a fool of himself." The story is centered on a touring puppet show, featuring the "Gold King," who attacks the protagonist to collect his eyes in a dream sequence. The setting of the encounter is unknown, but according to Edwards it "was Carcosa in an earlier draft." The use of rising action adds to the tension as well as the use of the "terminal climax."

If part of Edwards's horror style is the use of monsters we all know, the other is avoiding pastiche or imitation. While "A Certain Shade" has its genesis in Lovecraft's "Pickman's Model," it has its own voice in Edwards's mastery of a first-person narration to convey the theme of an artist's obsession in another tale of the karma of "cosmic vengeance."

One standard element of the collection is that all the stories display a strong sense of "point-of-attack," the moment in a story when the writer chooses to open the narrative. We come into these stories at the ripest moment, as evidenced in "We

Will Take Half." In this story we see the author's connection to his Texas origins with cultural delves into Latin American concerns with a mixture of pulp-era Robert E. Howard yarns and magical realism. The author believes that this tale "leans towards fantasy," but if it is fantasy it is used in a Harlan Ellison sort of way where the fantastic haunts us. Here the monster is loneliness and it can drive characters to seek resolutions that may be horrific.

The title track of this collection, "Whiskey and Memory," delivers on narrative description and works even more effectively on a second read. We follow the alcoholic John and his street wandering, which evokes the "urban horror" of Ramsey Campbell. The bulk of the narrative takes us into a strange medieval bar/nightclub, a purgatory of sorts for drinkers. If Charles Bukowski had written drunken horror this story would probably be it. The hallmarks of the tale are visually evocative descriptions and fluid changes in consciousness and time. The monster here is abuse—drug abuse and child abuse.

If there is any flaw in the collection it might be an overuse of a "sloshing" description when physical monsters make an appearance (even if only imaginary). The dialogue can sometimes be stilted or basic, and there is perhaps a repetitive use of the abusive parents motif. The collection is a little long, with stories like "Cabras" and "Volver Al Monte" essentially repeating the same themes. Even though together they serve as good examples of the folk horror trend, one of these stories would have sufficed.

Looking at the collection as a whole, it may prove difficult to classify many of these stories as traditional "supernatural horror" stories or just simply stories of "real-life horror." But that is the intersection Edward's collection is crossing with every story, and if horror stories in the weird tradition are human-centered at all, then this is the way to write them. In many of these characters, their internal horror toward themselves is as alienating as the cosmic indifference is to the rest of us. The collection shows a writer who has control of his skills and can apply them to the vast canvas of the horror genre. The stories do not allow themselves to be forgotten easily. They are 100% Sam L. Edwards.

Loving Horror Films Too Much

Acep Hale

JON KITLEY. *Discover the Horror: One Man's Quest for Monsters, Maniacs, and the Meaning of It All*. Chicago: Kitley's Krypt, 2019. 269 pp. $20.00 tpb. ISBN 978-0-9911279-1-7.

Right from the start I will say this book is a perfect example of why this world needs talented, dedicated editors. Jon Kitley's *Discover the Horror* is firmly within my wheelhouse: the memoir of a passionate horror fan who has turned his love for the genre into a second business for his family, a website with a long-standing and loyal following on the Internet, and an intellectual pursuit that has fulfilled him psychologically while unlocking a talent for writing he never believed himself capable of fulfilling. Yet as I read *Discover the Horror* I found myself wishing repeatedly that Kitley had an experienced editor or even a second reader divorced from the situation to push back against sections of this book. It's because I love books of this nature, and there's so much to love within *Discover the Horror,* that I really wanted this volume to have been polished like a jewel before it was sent to the printer.

Discover the Horror is broken into twenty-five chapters that start with Kitley's early childhood, his discovery of monster movies, his first forays into horror conventions, and the people and situations that pushed him to start a website. The table of contents goes on for more than a page and a half. I do not wish to take cheap shots, yet if your self-published book contains a foreword and an introduction, ponder long and hard over that old chestnut of writing, "spend twice as much time on editing as you do on writing." There's a chapter, "Chapter 6: Working in the Film Business," wherein Kitley describes his job as a teenage usher that, in my reading, does nothing to further his cause. I realize that in Jon's mind this chapter has gravity because this is where he met his wife, but to any reader without this emotional investment, the tale of how your sixteen-year-old self exercised his power over a twelve-year-old simply trying to sneak his friends into the theater comes across as unnecessary. This is one example where I'd be interested how the involvement of an experienced editor would have played in shaping the volume.

One area an editor would have been helpful is the amount of times Kitley goes off on tangents about his family's involvement in his passion. This is an early clue that *Discover the Horror* may have appeared as his one shot to express how much his wife and son mean to him; and while I appreciate the sentiment, after the fourth or fifth digression concerning his wife's involvement in the Kitley Turkey Day Marathon or his son meeting a B-movie legend my eyes began to glaze at these tales.

To clear the air, this book is not rife with typos. I realize this is the expectation when reviewers grouse about the need for an editor. *Discover the Horror* is not only admirably free of typos, it is free of spellchecked replacements that while spelled correctly are grammatically incorrect, which suggests that the people involved in the creation of this book poured blood, sweat, and tears into the project. One gets the feeling reading *Discover the Horror* that Jon Kitley believed that he was going to pour every last inch of his soul into its pages, and that's where our imaginary editor would have come into play. With someone to rein Kitley in, to curb his passion and say, "Jon, exclamation marks are akin to ghost-peppers. Capisce?," *Discover the Horror* would have easily shot to the top of my stacks.

So you know my tastes, I love Bill Landis's and Michelle Clifford's *Sleazoid Express,* which covers similar territory with the grindhouse fare of Times Square, and eagerly await each and every issue of Robin Bougie's *Cinema Sewer*. Whereas *Sleazoid Express* is obviously a finished endeavor due to Times Square's decline and fall, *Cinema Sewer* is a yearly publication by Canadian cartoonist Robin Bougie in which he illustrates and hand-letters his latest discoveries in the darker recesses of underground cinema and forgotten gems of yesteryear. I find *Cinema Sewer* so enjoyable that as I order each year's issue, I also order a back issue to complete my collection in addition to purchasing the collected volumes from FAB Press for when

I simply wish to kick back and go on an extended reading binge.

The reason I mention these titles is that I never feel as if I am being talked down to when reading *Sleazoid Express* or *Cinema Sewer*. Unfortunately, with *Discover the Horror* I frequently asked myself who was the intended audience of this book. My natural assumption would be that anyone interested in such a memoir would already have a baseline knowledge of the horror genre, yet Kitley frequently shifts into what I call "NPR downtalking" that verges on condescending in tone. By my calculations Kitley should be firmly within the Gen-X demographic; but good googly moogly, can he channel the Baby Boomer voice!

A prime example occurs early in the book when he regales the reader with the trials and tribulations of the pre-VCR days of broadcast television, bemoaning the fact that the kids of today simply don't know what it was like, when all media now lie at their beck and call. He then proceeds to waste a page explaining, in detail, the intricacies of *TV Guide*. Two things: I'm only five years younger than Kitley and I found this so frustrating I wanted to hurl the book across the room and abandon it then and there. Let's face it, if you grew up within the Gen-X population you know the deluge of articles that were written by Boomers about what slackers Gen-X were, how they didn't appreciate hard work, chose family and relationships over working overtime etc. etc. To watch members of Gen-X then turn around and join in on demonizing younger generations makes me seethe. Also, from a business point of view it simply doesn't make sense. Millennials and the younger Zoomers are rapidly outnumbering Boomers and Gen-X combined, and their embrace of fandom is both deeper and more encompassing. However, just to make sure, I checked and even Zoomers, much less the dreaded Millennials, are well aware of *TV Guide*. Second, since Kitley had just written at length about how easy it is for people to access data, it stands to reason that if his readers didn't know what a *TV Guide* was they'd simply pick up their phones and type seven characters into a search engine, negating the need for the NPR downtalking.

Not to beat a dead horse, and I don't want to give the impression I hated this book, yet I feel Kitley overstates the ease of finding films in this day and age. Agreed, the films he writes of are relatively easy to find, yet if you read *Cinema Sewer* and *Weng's Chop,* or watch Tanner's YouTube channel *Unboxed, Watched and Reviewed,* you know there are a great many of films that are well-nigh impossible to get your hands on even with good connections on pirating and trading forums. This is another time where I found myself questioning who, precisely, was the audience for this book. It seems to fit the Boomer nostalgia mold, yet it takes strange turns when Kitley begins talking down to readers, telling them how to be good stewards of the genre, giving advice to beginning collectors, and offering steps to becoming a good horror fan.

I wish to get all this out of the way, because I'm one of those people who always want to know the bad news first, to rip the Band-Aid off quickly. Obviously, if I didn't enjoy the hell out of this book, I wouldn't have spent all the above paragraphs going, "And another thing . . ." Or maybe I would. Maybe I have discovered the horror. Seriously, though, there is a lot to love in this book. Right out of the gate there's the passion. It's clear from the beginning that Kitley has an all-consuming love for the horror genre in all its manifestations and is unafraid to show it. There is no hedging of bets or offerings of caveats with Kitley, and this is a relief. This man is unapologetic in his love for horror, and it simply makes you want to stand and high-five empty air several times per chapter. For every point I found myself in disagreement with Kitley there were at least five when I found myself saying aloud, "Oh, hell yes." Kitley would fit right in on my front stoop or at my corner bar, able to hold his own in a free-for-all, far-ranging conversation that delves into esoteric pockets of our shared interests.

I found common ground with Kitley in his chapter regarding his early and lifelong fascination with Frankenstein's monster. With the two hundredth anniversary of the publication of *Frankenstein* having occurred last year, there is a possibility that we're all sympathetically attuned to Mary Shelley's creation; yet, as Kitley points out, her monster plucks a uniquely resonant string within outsider children. I remarked to my wife recently that as a kid I was attracted to the comic book characters of the Hulk and the Thing because of my earlier reading of Victor Hugo's *The Hunchback of Notre Dame,* another character Kitley points out as being attractive to outsiders.

In another early chapter Kitley describes the process for his transformation into a "Cinematic Archaeologist," his term for one who becomes so interested with films he begins reading articles, magazines, journals, and books in addition to viewing as many films as possible in order to heighten his knowledge and thus his appreciation of the films he is watching. One of my favorite books is William Castle's *Step Right Up! I'm Going to Scare the Pants Off America,* not only for the background information on Castle's films but the pure grift sense by which Castle operated and the manner in which he was able to convey the spirit of the times in which he worked. Castle was crafting films in an era during which the studio system was still finding its way. There were cracks in the system the cunning could exploit, and Castle was working angles on any he could find. In writing *Step Right Up!* Castle gifts us with a clearer portrait of Hollywood than we're likely to find in either the sanitized versions approved by TCM or those designed to titillate à la *Hollywood Babylon*. In a similar manner, *Discover the Horror* offers a fascinating snapshot of convention culture before it became an industry unto itself, as Kitley reminisces about his first tentative forays attending conventions and his deepening engagement with the subcultures within these scattered gatherings.

We can never know what future generations will find valuable. I once made my living as a magician. My shows traced the history of magic along with performances of the illusions being discussed and their social implications. Magic, being a performative art whose history largely prefigures the invention of film, requires historians and sociologists to turn to playbills, performers' and audience members' diaries, and other accumulated ephemera in an attempt to assemble a documentary montage of the effect magic had upon its viewers and its wider societies. Of course, it should surprise no one that it was the French that were at the vanguard of this movement and still hold this position today. However, I wonder if the people returning from a cheap night out to watch a raucous revue ever knew the importance those hastily scrawled entries may prove to future generations.

Just as we assume all media lie at our fingertips (to be fair, later in the book Kitley does write of the importance of showing enthusiasm for older, obscure films to keep them available), there is also a mistaken belief that everything written on the Internet will remain available for all time. Yet companies such as Facebook have refused the Internet Archive access in order to digitally store what its patrons publish on the platform. As companies such as Facebook continue to expand their user base, maintain this policy of not allowing outside archival services access, and inevitably wane and decline as do all such companies, that information may be lost forever. While we can still access Angelfire, Geocities, and Tripod sites exactly as they once were, the majority of Web 2.0 as we now know it will one day cease to exist.

Books such as *Discover the Horror* may prove invaluable to future generations as a snapshot of this era, which still exists once the digital remnants have disappeared into the ether. Here lies my dilemma, because on the one hand I could spend too many words covering the variety of topics Kitley writes about in this book, yet on the other hand, as I said at the beginning, I truly wish he'd had someone working alongside to rein him in. I harbor a suspicion that the bare bones of *Discover the Horror* originated with posts Kitley published on his website, which, though they were polished, leads to a degree of overlap within *Discover the Horror*'s twenty-five chapters. With the benefit of an editor he'd have someone to assist in tightening the focus of the work, perhaps break the book into two separate volumes, and by heightening the attention of those works he'd have a pair of lean, efficient books that repaid a higher value for their reader's involvement.

The very last thing I desire is for anyone to think I did not enjoy reading this book. It's only because I love this kind of work so dearly that I really want to see it presented in the best possible light. My gold standard for this type of book remains Joel Lane's *This Spectacular Darkness,* because Joel took each creator he chose to address and approached them fresh, abandoning all critical writing on their canon, working his way through the important works of their oeuvre to see how he himself felt, and then producing his own personal essay on the artist in question which bore all the marks and quirks of his personality. It's impossible to separate Lane's personal vision from those essays. and by the end of *This Spectacular Darkness* you feel as if you know Lane, though he did not spend chapters expounding upon his personal biography.

Yet at the same time I fully acknowledge I hold no crystal ball. It may well be that the precise points I kvetch about in this writing are what future readers find of most importance. In the end, I can only write of my feelings, and to me *Discover the Horror* feels akin to a lifetime of emotion, turmoil, and passion that Kitley saw as possibly his one and only chance to get on the page and into the world. If I'm wrong in this impression, then I apologize. If I'm right, then my admittedly flawed and limited advice would be take a well-deserved victory lap, high-five the world, and get your ass back to the keyboard. Your genre needs your voice, and now that you've relieved that pressure you can relax into the writing. You've proven you have the skills and devotion.

Haters and Devotees Alike: NecronomiCon 2019

Geza A. G. Reilly

The frankly ridiculous acrimony between Lovecraft "haters" and Lovecraft "devotees" could be put to bed by NecronomiCon 2019. Though I was unable to attend every piece of programming, I did intentionally keep myself as busy as possible, and I kept an eye out for moments of disrespect toward Lovecraft or his work. I am pleased to report that for the vast majority of my time in Providence, nothing but respect was shown to the Old Gentleman.

This is not to say that the more difficult aspects of Lovecraft's life were left out. Lovecraft's flaws were discussed with candor during panels, leading the participants and the audience to a greater understanding of his life, writing, and genre. At no point were these discussions anything but honest about the facts of the matter, and though obviously Lovecraft's poorer opinions were rejected, the man himself was never unnecessarily denigrated. The worst point of the panels was when a speaker (myself) suggested that if weird fiction were to continue its tradition of rejecting previously used tropes, then perhaps modern weird fiction must reject Lovecraftian tropes themselves. (In my defense, I did preface it by saying that the thought made me feel like a traitor!)

The events were a smorgasbord of worship for Lovecraft. From the opening ceremony, wonderfully interrupted by the traditional playing of "Yes, We Have No Bananas," to the closing convention committee discussion, Lovecraft—especially his sense of play—loomed over us all. No eyebrows were raised over any past offensive outgrowths from the material being enjoyed, nor were there any stern enforcers ensuring that Theobald received his due. Instead, all attendees enjoyed the songs, the shows, the raucous participation, and everything else that was offered in Lovecraft's name.

I can think of only two events that stood out as questionable. One was an attendee at the closing panel who claimed that Lovecraft was a bad writer. That individual was met with silence, neither dismissing nor endorsing what they said. The other was a committee member who commented that Lovecraft was somewhat of an albatross around the convention's neck. This was excusable, however, since his larger point was that the convention, born out of Lovecraftian fandom, should be able to explore other areas of horror. This was an understandable concern, since a hyper-focused convention is bound to run dry of ideas eventually.

The acrimony over NecronomiCon was something that I had thought left behind since 2017. I was dismayed to see that it was beginning again in Lovecraftian circles in advance of the convention. My reminiscence of NecronomiCon 2019, therefore, is the relief I felt at the end of the weekend, as I dragged myself back to the hotel after seeing *The Dunwich Horror,* that the reigniting of old fights had seemingly been left at the door. It left me hopeful that, in the wake of so much upset over the past two years, we might at last be able to leave our petty disagreements where they belong: discarded and forgotten.

About the Contributors

Michael Abolafia is a co-editor of *Dead Reckonings*.

Marc Aramini was born of military parents but has spent most of his life in the American Southwest. His most notable work involves the science fiction writer Gene Wolfe. Though he has worked in banks, gyms, and even a traveling Spanish-speaking circus, he currently teaches college English.

Ramsey Campbell is an English horror fiction writer, editor, and critic who has been writing for well over fifty years. He is frequently cited as one of the leading writers in the field. His web- site is www.ramseycampbell.com.

Peter Cannon is a senior editor at *Publishers Weekly,* assigning and editing the reviews in the Mystery/Thriller category. He is also the author of *H. P. Lovecraft,* a critical study in Twayne's United States Authors Series, and other works related to Lovecraft.

Greg Gbur is a professor of physics and optical science at UNCC Charlotte. For more than a decade he has written a blog called *Skulls in the Stars* (https://skullsinthestars.com) about physics, horror fiction, and curious intersections between them. He has written a number of introductions to classic reprinted horror novels for Valancourt Books.

Fiona Maeve Geist lives with her cat in WXXT country, where she freelances RPGs and writes short fiction. Her work has appeared in *Lamplight Quarterly,* CLASH Media, *Mothership* (RPG), and *Ashes and Entropy*.

Edward Guimont recently received his Ph.D. from the University of Connecticut's Department of History.

Acep Hale is a magician, comedian, and writer who currently resides in Brooklyn, New York.

Alex Houstoun is a co-editor of *Dead Reckonings*.

S. T. Joshi is the author of such critical studies as *The Weird Tale* (1990), *H. P. Lovecraft: The Decline of the West* (1990), and *Unutterable Horror: A History of Supernatural Fiction* (2012). He has prepared corrected editions of H. P. Lovecraft's work for Arkham House and annotated editions of the weird tales of Lovecraft, Algernon Blackwood, Lord Dunsany, M. R. James, Arthur Machen, and Clark Ashton Smith for Penguin Classics, as well as the anthology *American Supernatural Tales* (2007).

Karen Joan Kohoutek, an independent scholar and poet, has published about weird fiction in various journals and literary websites. Recent and upcoming publications have been on subjects including the Gamera films, the Robert E. Howard/H. P. Lovecraft correspondence, folk magic in the novels of Ishmael Reed, and the proto-Gothic writer Charles Brockden Brown. She lives in Fargo, North Dakota.

Michael D. Miller is an adjunct professor and NEH medievalist summer scholar with numerous one-act play productions, awards, including several optioned screenplays to his credit. He is the author of the *Realms of Fantasy RPG* for Mythopoeia Games Publications. His poetry has appeared *Spectral Realms* and his scholarly publications in *Lovecraft Annual*.

Daniel Pietersen is a writer of weird fiction and horror philosophy. He has a blog of fragmentary work and other thoughts at https://constantuniversity.wordpress.com.

Géza A. G. Reilly is a writer and critic with an interest in twentieth-century American genre literature. A Canadian expatriate, he now lives in the wilds of Florida with his wife, Andrea, and their cat, Mim.

Darrell Schweitzer is an American writer, editor, and critic in the field of speculative fiction. Much of his focus has been on dark fantasy and horror, although he does also work in science fiction and fantasy.

Donald Sidney-Fryer is a poet, historian, entertainer, and one of the foremost experts on the work of Clark Ashton

Smith. His latest book, *West of Wherevermore and Other Essays,* was published by Hippocampus Press.

Farah Rose Smith is a poet, fiction writer, musician, and artist whose work often focuses on the Gothic and surreal. She is the founder and editor of *Mantid Magazine,* a publication promoting women and diverse writers in weird fiction, and also the founder of Grimoire Pictures, a small art film company.

Michelle Souliere works in the bookmines at the Green Hand Bookshop in Portland, Maine, occasionally emerging from the vasty bookdeeps to scrawl charcoal, pencil, and ink on any surface she can find. She is also the author of the book *Strange Maine: True Tales from the Pine Tree State.*

Elena Tchougounova-Paulson has worked as head of the Communications Department and later as a research fellow and publisher at the Research Information Centre at the Russian State Archive of Literature and Art, Moscow. She is now an independent researcher, residing in Cambridge.

Bev Vincent is the author of several books. His work has been nominated for the Bram Stoker Award (twice), the Edgar Award, and the ITW Thriller Award, and he won the 2010 Al Blanchard Award. His reviews also appear at *Onyx Reviews* (onyxreviews.com). He is a contributing editor with *Cemetery Dance* and has published more than eighty short stories. His web presence is bevvincent.com.

Hank Wagner is a respected critic and journalist. Among the many publications in which his work regularly appears are *Cemetery Dance* and *Mystery Scene*.

CPSIA information can be obtained
at www.ICGtesting.com
Printed in the USA
BVHW040924230720
584315BV00006B/143